# Dancers
*in the*
# Dark
&
# Layla
# Steps Up

# Dancers
## *in the*
# Dark
— *&* —
# Layla
# Steps Up

## THE LAYLA COLLECTION

## *Charlaine Harris*

Subterranean Press 2020

# TABLE *of* CONTENTS

# ACKNOWLEDGMENTS

MY THANKS to dancers past and present:

Coco Ihle, Larry Roquemore, Jo Dierdorff, Shelley Freydont and the very helpful Molly McBride.

Special thanks go to Doris Ann Norris, reference librarian to the stars, who can look up the inner dimensions of a sarcophagus faster than I can whistle "Dixie."

# INTRODUCTION

THESE TWO STORIES about Layla and her dance partner are the only ones that were destined from the beginning to be romantic. A long time ago, an editor at *Harlequin* asked me to write a novella. Since I'd written books that contained relationships but weren't truly under the Romance umbrella, I thought I'd give it a try. "Dancers in the Dark" was the result. It was originally packaged with novellas by Laurell K. Hamilton and Barbara Hambly. In later years, *Harlequin* repackaged "Dancers" with works by other writers. It's been the little novella that chugged along.

When the rights reverted to me, I welcomed the opportunity to write about Layla again. I wanted her character to have grown in the interim between "Dancers in the Dark" and "Layla Steps Up." I figured it was time for Layla to do the saving, rather than being saved. And she's jolted out of her passivity by discovering that the vampire community does not exactly have a Layla fan club.

Oddly enough, though these are short works, I had to do more research for them than I normally have to do for full-length books.

And as usually happens, I could only put a little bit of what I learned about dancing into the finished work.

It was tremendous fun writing something that felt new to me, and I've always enjoyed writing novellas and short stories. Maybe some day I'll return to Layla to check on her happiness.

Charlaine Harris

# Dancers
*in the*
## Dark

# CHAPTER ONE

R UE PAUSED TO gather herself before she pushed open
the door marked both Blue Moon Entertainment and
Black Moon Productions. She'd made sure she'd be right on time
for her appointment. Desperation clamped down on her like a
vise: she had to get this job, even if the conditions were distasteful. Not only would the money make continuing her university
courses possible, the job hours dovetailed with her classes. *Okay,
head up, chest out, shoulders square, big smile, pretty hands,* Rue told
herself, as her mother had told her a thousand times.

There were two men—two vampires, she corrected herself—one dark, one red-haired, and a woman, a regular human
woman, waiting for her. In the corner, at a barre, a girl with short
blond hair was stretching. The girl might be eighteen, three years
younger than Rue.

The older woman was hard-faced, expensively dressed, perhaps forty. Her pantsuit had cost more than three of Rue's outfits,
at least the ones that she wore to classes every day. She thought of
those outfits as costumes: old jeans and loose shirts bought at the

thrift store, sneakers or hiking boots and big glasses with a very weak prescription. She was concealed in such an ensemble at this moment, and Rue realized from the woman's face that her appearance was an unpleasant surprise.

"You must be Rue?" the older woman asked.

Rue nodded, extended her hand. "Rue May. Pleased to meet you." Two lies in a row. It was getting to be second nature—or even (and this was what scared her most) first nature.

"I'm Sylvia Dayton. I own Blue Moon Entertainment and Black Moon Productions." She shook Rue's hand in a firm, brisk way.

"Thank you for agreeing to see me dance." Rue crammed her apprehension into a corner of her mind and smiled confidently. She'd endured the judgments of strangers countless times. "Where do I change?" She let her gaze skip right over the vampires—her potential partners, she guessed. At least they were both taller than her own five foot eight. In the hasty bit of research she'd done, she'd read that vampires didn't like to shake hands, so she didn't offer. Surely she was being rude in not even acknowledging their presence? But Sylvia hadn't introduced them.

"In there." There were some louver-doored enclosures on one side of the room, much like changing rooms in a department store. Rue entered a cubicle. It was easy to slide out of the oversize clothes and the battered lace-up boots, a real pleasure to pull on black tights, a deep plum leotard and fluttering wrap skirt to give the illusion of a dress while she danced. She sat on a stool to put on T-strap heels, called character shoes, then stood to smile experimentally at her reflection in the mirror. *Head up, chest out, shoulders square, big smile, pretty hands,* she repeated silently. Rue took the clip out of her hair and brushed it until it fell in a heavy curtain past her shoulder blades. Her hair was one of her best features. It was a deep, rich brown with an undertone of auburn. The color almost matched that of her deep-set, dramatic eyes.

Rue only needed her glasses to clarify writing on the blackboard, so she popped them into their case and slipped it into her backpack. She leaned close to the mirror to inspect her makeup. After years of staring into her mirror with the confidence of a beautiful girl, she now examined her face with the uncertainty of a battered woman. There were pictures in a file at her lawyer's office, pictures of her face bruised and puffy. Her nose—well, it looked fine now.

The plastic surgeon had done a great job.

So had the dentist.

Her smile faltered, dimmed. She straightened her back again. She couldn't afford to think about that now. It was show time. She folded back the door and stepped out.

There was a moment of silence as the four in the room took in Rue's transformation. The darker vampire looked gratified; the red-haired one's expression didn't change. That pleased Rue.

"You were fooling us," Sylvia said. She had a deep, raspy voice. "You were in disguise." *I'd better remember that Sylvia Dayton is perceptive,* Rue told herself. "Well, let's try you on the dance floor, since you definitely pass in the looks department. By the way, it's Blue Moon you want to try out for, right? Not Black Moon? You could do very well in a short time with Black Moon, with your face and body."

It was Blue Moon's ad she'd answered. "Dancer wanted, must work with vamps, have experience, social skills," the ad had read. "Salary plus tips."

"What's the difference?" Rue asked.

"Black Moon, well, you have to be willing to have sex in public."

Rue couldn't remember the last time she'd been shocked, but she was shocked now. "No!" she said, trying not to sound as horrified as she felt. "And if this tryout has anything to do with removing my clothes..."

"No, Blue Moon Entertainment is strictly for dancing," Sylvia said. She was calm about it. "As the ad said, you team with a vampire. That's what the people want these days. Whatever kind of dancing the party calls for—waltzing, hip-hop. The tango is very popular. People just want a dance team to form the centerpiece for their evening, get the party started. They like the vamp to bite the girl at the end of the exhibition dance."

She'd known that; it had been in the ad, too. All the material she'd read had told her it didn't hurt badly, and the loss of a sip of blood wouldn't affect her. She'd been hurt worse.

"After you dance as a team, often you're required to stay for an hour, dancing with the guests," Sylvia was saying. "Then you go home. They pay me a fee. I pay you. Sometimes you get tips. If you agree to anything on the side and I hear about it, you're fired." It took Rue a minute to understand what Sylvia meant, and her mouth compressed. Sylvia continued. "Pretty much the same arrangement applies for Black Moon, but the entertainment is different, and the pay is higher. We're thinking of adding vampire jugglers and a vampire magician—he'll need a 'Beautiful Assistant.'"

It steadied Rue somehow when she realized that Sylvia was simply being matter-of-fact. Sex performer, magician's assistant or dancer, Sylvia didn't care.

"Blue Moon," Rue said firmly.

"Blue Moon it is," Sylvia said.

The blond girl drifted over to stand by Sylvia. She had small hazel eyes and a full mouth that was meant to smile. She wasn't smiling now.

While Sylvia searched through a stack of CD cases, the blonde stepped up to Rue's side. She whispered, "Don't look directly in their eyes. They can snag you that way, if they want to, turn your will to their wishes. Don't worry unless their fangs run all the way out. They're excited then."

Startled, Rue used her lowest voice to say, "Thanks!" But now she was even more nervous, and she had to wonder if perhaps that hadn't been the girl's intention.

Having picked a CD, Sylvia tapped the arm of one of the vampires. "Thompson, you first."

The dark-haired taller vampire, who was wearing biking shorts and a ragged, sleeveless T-shirt, came to stand in front of Rue. He was very handsome, very exotic, with golden skin and smooth short hair. Rue guessed he was of Eurasian heritage; there was a hint of a slant to his dark eyes. He smiled down at her. But there was something in his look she didn't trust, and she always paid attention to that feeling…at least, now she did. After a quick scan of his face, she kept her eyes focused on his collarbone.

Rue had never touched a vampire. Where she came from, a smallish town in Tennessee, you never saw anything so exotic. If you wanted to see a vampire (just like if you wanted to go to the zoo), you had to visit the city. The idea of touching a dead person made Rue queasy. She would have been happy to turn on her heel and walk right out of the room, but that option wasn't open. Her savings had run out. Her rent was due. Her phone bill was imminent. She had no insurance.

She heard her mother's voice in her head, reminding her, "Put some steel in that spine, honey." Good advice. Too bad her mother hadn't followed it herself.

Sylvia popped the disk in the CD player, and Rue put one hand on Thompson's shoulder, extended the other in his grasp. His hands were cool and dry. This partner would never have sweaty palms. She tried to suppress her shiver. *You don't have to like a guy to dance with him,* she advised herself. The music was an almost generic dance tune. They began with a simple two-step, then a box step. The music accelerated into swing, progressed to jitterbug.

Rue found she could almost forget her partner was a vampire. Thompson could really dance. And he was so strong! He could lift her with ease, swing her, toss her over his head, roll her across his back. She felt light as a feather. But she hadn't mistaken the gleam in his eyes. Even while they were dancing, his hands traveled over more of her body than they should. She'd had enough experience with men—more than enough experience—to predict the way their partnership would go, if it began like this.

The music came to an end. He watched her chest move up and down from the exercise. He wasn't even winded. Of course, she reminded herself, Thompson didn't need to breathe. The vampire bowed to Rue, his eyes dancing over her body. "A pleasure," he said. To her surprise, his voice purely American.

She nodded back.

"Excellent," Sylvia said. "You two look good together. Thompson, Julie, you can go now, if you want." The blonde and Thompson didn't seem to want. They both sat down on the floor, backs to one of the huge mirrors that lined the room. "Now dance with Sean O'Rourke, our Irish aristocrat," Sylvia told her. "He needs a new partner, too." Rue must have looked anxious, because the older woman laughed and said, "Sean's partner got engaged and left the city. Thompson's finished med school and started her residency. Sean?"

The second vampire stepped forward, and Rue realized he hadn't moved the whole time she'd been dancing with Thompson. Now he gave Sylvia a frigid nod and examined Rue as closely as she was examining him.

Dust could have settled on Sean, he stood so still. He was shorter than Thompson, but still perhaps two inches taller than Rue, and his long straight hair, tied back at the nape of his neck, was bright red. Of course, Sean was white, white as paper; Thompson's racial heritage, his naturally golden skin, had made him look a little more alive.

The Irish vampire's mouth was like a capital M. The graven downturns made him look a little spoiled, a little petulant, but it was just the way his mouth was made. She wondered what he would look like if he ever smiled. Sean's eyes were blue and clear, and he had a dusting of freckles across his sharp nose. A vampire with freckles—that made Rue want to laugh. She ducked her head to hide her smile as he took his stance in front of her.

"I am amusing?" he asked, so softly she was sure the other three couldn't hear.

"Not at all," she said, but she couldn't suppress her smile.

"Have you ever talked to a vampire?"

"No. Oh, wait, yes, I have. A beauty contest I was in, I think maybe Miss Rockland Valley? He was one of the judges."

Of all the ways Sean the vampire could have responded, he said, "Did you win?"

She raised her eyes and looked directly into his. He could not have looked more bored and indifferent. It was strangely reassuring. "I did," she said.

She remembered the vampire judge's sardonic smile when she'd told him her "platform" was governmental tolerance toward supernatural creatures. And yet she'd never met a supernatural creature until that moment! What a naive twit she'd been. But her mother had thought such a topic very current and sure to attract the judges' attention. National and state governments had been struggling to regulate human-vampire relationships since vampires had announced their existence among humans five years before.

The Japanese development of a synthetic blood that could satisfy the nutritional needs of the undead had made such a revelation possible, and in the past five years, vampires had worked their way into the mainstream of society in a few countries. But Rue, despite her platform, had steered clear of contact with the undead. Her life was troublesome enough without adding an element as volatile as the undead to the mix.

"I just don't know much about vampires," she said apologetically.

Sean's crystalline blue eyes looked at her quite impersonally. "Then you will learn," he said calmly. He had a slight Irish accent; "learn" came out suspiciously like "lairrn."

She focused safely on his pointed chin. She felt more at ease—even if he was some kind of royalty, according to Sylvia. He seemed totally indifferent to her looks. That, in itself, was enough to relax her muscles.

"Will you dance?" he asked formally.

"Yes, thank you," she said automatically. Sylvia started the CD player again. She'd picked a different disk this time.

They waltzed first, moving so smoothly that Rue felt she was gliding across the floor without her feet touching the wood. "Swing next," he murmured, and her feet did truly leave the floor, her black skirt fluttering out in an arc, and then she was down again and dancing.

Rue enjoyed herself more than she had in years.

When it was over, when she saw that his eyes were still cool and impersonal, it was easy to turn to Sylvia and say, "If you decide you want me to work for you, I'd like to dance with Sean."

The flash of petulance on Thompson's face startled Rue.

Sylvia looked a bit surprised, but not displeased. "Great," she said. "It's not always easy…" Then she stopped, realizing any way she finished the sentence might be tactless.

Julie was beaming. "Then I'll dance with Thompson," she said. "I need a partner, too."

*At least I made Julie happy*, Rue thought. Rue's own partner-to-be didn't comment. Sean looked neither happy nor sad. He took her hand, bowed over it and let it go. She thought she had felt cold lips touch her fingers, and she shivered.

"Here's the drill," Sylvia said briskly. "Here's a contract for you to sign. Take it home with you and read it. It's really simple." She handed Rue a one-page document. "You can have your lawyer check it over, if you want."

Rue couldn't afford that, but she nodded, hoping her face didn't reflect her thoughts.

"We have personnel meetings once a month, Blue Moon and Black Moon together," Sylvia said. "You have to come to those. If you don't show up for an engagement, and you're not in the hospital with a broken leg, you're fired. If you fight with Sean, it better not show in public."

"What are the meetings for?" Rue asked.

"We need to know one another by sight," Sylvia said. "And we need to share problems we have with clients. You can avoid a lot of situations if you know who's going to be trouble."

It was news to Rue that there could be "trouble." She crossed her arms over her chest, suddenly feeling cold in the plum leotard. Then she looked down at the contract and saw what she would be paid per appearance. She knew that she'd sign; she'd have the contract in Sylvia's hands the next day, so she could start work as soon as possible.

But after she'd gotten back to her cheap apartment, which lay in a decidedly unsafe part of Rhodes, Rue did study the contract. Nothing in the simple language was a surprise; everything was as Sylvia had told her. There were a few more rules, covering items like giving notice and maintaining any costumes she borrowed from the company stock, but the contract was basic. It was renewable, if both parties wanted, after a year.

The next morning, Rue bundled up in the brisk midwest spring morning and set out early to the campus so she would have time to detour. There was a mail slot in the door of the old building that housed Blue Moon/Black Moon. Rue poked the folded paper through the slit, feeling profound relief. That night Sylvia called Rue to schedule her first practice session with Sean O'Rourke.

# CHAPTER TWO

WEARING CUTOFF SWEATPANTS and a sleeveless T-shirt, Sean waited in the studio. The new woman wasn't late yet. She would be on time. She needed the job. He'd followed her home the night she'd auditioned. He'd been cautious all the years he'd been a vampire, and that had kept him alive for more than 275 years. One of his safety measures was making sure to know the people he dealt with, so Sean was determined to learn more about this Rue.

He didn't know what to think of her. She was poor, obviously. But she'd had years of dance lessons; she'd had good makeup, a good haircut, the good English of privilege. Could she be an undercover operative of some kind? If she were, wouldn't she have taken the opportunity to work for Black Moon, the only remotely interesting thing about Sylvia's enterprises? Perhaps she was a rich girl on a perverse adventure.

His first fifty years as a vampire, Sean O'Rourke had done his best to conceal himself in the world of humans. He'd stayed away from others of his kind; when he was with them, the temptation to explore his true nature had grown too strong. Sean had been abandoned by the man who'd made him what he was. He'd had no chance to learn the basic rules of his condition; in his ignorance, he'd killed unfortunates in the slums of Dublin. Gradually, Sean had learned that killing his victims wasn't necessary. A mouthful of blood could sustain him, if he had it every night. He'd learned to use his vampiric influence to blot out his victims' memories, and he'd learned to blot out his own emotions almost as successfully.

After fifty years, stronger and colder, he'd begun to risk the company of other vampires. He'd fallen in love a time or two, and it had always ended badly, whether the woman he loved was another vampire or a human.

His new partner, this Rue, was beautiful, one of the most beautiful women he'd seen in centuries. Sean could admire that beauty without being swayed by it. He knew something was wrong with the girl, something hidden inside her. He hadn't watched people, observed people, all these years without learning to tell when a human was concealing something. Maybe she was an agent for one of the fanatical organizations that had formed to force vampires back into the darkness of the shadows. Maybe she suffered from a drug addiction, or some physical condition she was hoping to hide for as long as possible.

Sean shrugged to himself. He'd speculated far too much about Rue's possibilities. Whatever her secret was, in time he would learn it. He wasn't looking forward to the revelation. He wanted to dance with her for a long time; she was light and supple in his arms, and she smelled good, and the swing of her thick mahogany hair made something in his chest ache.

Though he tried to deny it to himself, Sean looked forward to tasting her more than he'd looked forward to anything in decades.

———◆———

THE PRACTICE room was a larger studio behind the room in which she'd met Sylvia and the others. "Sean/Rue" was scrawled on the sign-up sheet for the six-thirty to eight o'clock time slot. Julie and Thompson would be practicing after them, Rue noticed.

She was nervous about being alone with the vampire. He was waiting for her, just as still and silent as he'd been two nights before. As a precaution, she'd worn a cross around her neck, tucked under the old gray leotard. The black shorts she'd pulled on over the leotard were made out of a shiny synthetic, and she'd brought ballet shoes, tap shoes and the T-strap character shoes she wore for ballroom dancing. She nodded to Sean by way of greeting, and she dumped the shoes out on the floor. "I didn't know what you'd want," she explained, all too aware that her voice was uneven.

"Why are the initials different?" he asked. Even his voice sounded dusty, as though it hadn't been used in years. To her dismay, Rue discovered that she found the slight Irish accent charming.

"What do you mean? Oh, on the shoe bag?" She sounded like an idiot, she thought, and bit her lip. She'd had the shoe bag for so many years, she simply didn't notice anymore that it was monogrammed.

"What is your real name?"

She risked a glance upward. The brilliant blue eyes were just blue eyes; they were fixed on her at the moment, but he wasn't trying to rope her in, or whatever it was they did. "It's a secret," she said, like a child. She smacked herself on the forehead.

"What is your true name?" He still sounded calm, but it was clear he was going to insist. Actually, Rue didn't blame him. She met his eyes. She was his partner. He should know.

"I go by Rue L. May. My name is Layla LaRue LeMay. My parents liked the song? You know it?" she asked doubtfully.

"Which version? The original one by Cream, or the slower Eric Clapton solo?"

She smiled, though it was an uncertain smile. "Original," she said. "In their wilder years, they thought it was cool to name their daughter after a song." It was hard to believe, now, that her parents had ever had years of not being afraid what people would think, that once they'd been whimsical. She looked down. "Please don't tell anyone my name."

"I won't." She believed him. "Where do your parents live now?" he asked.

"They're dead," she said, and he knew she was lying.

And though he would need to sample her blood to be sure, Sean also suspected that his new partner was living in fear.

———————◆———————

AFTER THEY warmed up, that first practice session went fairly well. As long as they both concentrated on the dancing, the conversation was easy. When they touched on anything more personal, it wasn't.

Sean explained that they were almost never called on to tap dance. "People who hire us want something flashy, or something romantic," he said. "They want a couple who can tango, or a couple who can do big lifts, for the charity balls. If it's something like an engagement party or anniversary, they want a sexy, slow dance, always ending with the bite."

Rue admired how impersonally he said it, as if they were both professionals in this together, like actors rehearsing a scene. In fact, that was exactly appropriate, she decided.

"I've never done this," she said. "The biting thing. Ah, do you always bite the neck?" As if she didn't care, as if she was quite matter-of-fact about the finale. She was proud of how calm she sounded.

"That's what the audience likes. They can see it best, and it's traditional. In real life, of course—if I can use the phrase 'real life'—we can bite anywhere. The neck and the groin have the big arteries, so they're preferred. It isn't fatal. I'll only take a drop or two. We don't need much as we get older."

Rue could feel her face flood with color. This matched what she'd learned from the university's computers, though she'd felt obliged to have Sean confirm what she'd read. She needed to know all this, but she was embarrassed, just the same. It was like discussing sexual positions, rather than the more comparable eating customs: missionary vs. doggy-style, rather than forks vs. chopsticks.

"Let's try a tango," Sean said. Rue put on her character shoes. "Can you wear a higher heel?" her partner asked impersonally.

"Yes, I can dance in something higher, but that would put me too close to your height, don't you think?"

"I'm not proud," he said simply. "It's all in how it looks."

Aristocrat or not, he was a practical man. To Rue's pleasure, Sean continued to be a great partner. He was very professional.

He was patient, and since she was rusty, she appreciated his forbearance. As the session continued, Rue grew more confident. Her body began to recover its skills, and she began to enjoy herself immensely.

She hadn't had fun in forever.

They ended up with a "cool-down" dance, a dreamy forties romantic song performed by a big band. As the music came to a close, Sean said, "Now I'll dip you." Then he lowered her, until her back was almost parallel with the floor. And he held the position. A human couldn't have sustained it for long, but his arm under her shoulders was like iron. All she had to do was keep her graceful alignment with his body. "Then, I bite," he said, and mimed a nip at her neck. He felt her shiver and willed her to relax. But she didn't, and after a moment, he assisted her in standing up again.

"We could have a booking this weekend, if you feel you're up to it," he said. "We'd have to practice every night, and you'd have to have your costumes ready."

She was relieved to have a safe topic to latch on to. Julie and Thompson were standing by the door, waiting for their turn in the practice room. They were listening with interest.

"Sylvia said there was a wardrobe of costumes?"

"I'll show you," Sean said. He sounded as calm and indifferent as he had at the beginning of the session.

After she'd glanced in the room off Sylvia's office, where costumes were hanging in rows on rolling racks, she went to the ladies' room. As she was washing her hands, Julie came in. The young blonde looked especially happy, with flushed cheeks and a big smile.

"I gotta tell you," Julie said. "I'm really glad you picked Sean. I always thought Thompson was pretty hot, and Sean is as cold as they come."

"How long have you been dancing for Sylvia?" Rue asked. She wanted to steer clear of discussing her partner.

"Oh, a year. I have a day job, too, clerking at an insurance agency, but you know how hard it is to get along. I settled in Rhodes because I thought a city in the middle of the country would be cheaper than either coast, but it's hard for a girl to make it on her own."

Rue was able to agree with that wholeheartedly.

"Hard to understand why the vampires do this," she said.

"They gotta live, too. I mean, most of them, they want a nice place to live, clean clothes and so on."

"I guess I always thought all vampires were rich."

"Not to hear them tell it. Besides, Thompson's only been a vamp for twenty years."

"Wow," Rue said. She had no idea what difference that would make, but Julie clearly thought she was revealing a significant fact.

"He's pretty low down on the totem pole," Julie explained. "What's unusual is finding a vamp as old as Sean performing. Most of the vamps that old think it's beneath their dignity to work for a human." She looked a wee bit contemptuous of Sean.

Rue said, "You all have a good practice, Julie. I'll see you soon."

"Sure," Julie said. "Have a good week."

Rue hadn't meant to be abrupt. But she had some sympathy for Sean. Just like her, he was making a living doing what he did best, and he didn't have false pride about it. She could draw a lesson from that herself.

That sympathy vanished the next night, when Rue discovered that Sean was following her home. After getting off the bus, she caught the barest glimpse of him as she walked the last block to her apartment. She ran up the steps as quickly as she could, and tried to act normally as she unlocked the common door and climbed up to her tiny apartment. Slamming the door behind her, her heart hammering, she wondered what she'd let herself in for. With the greatest caution, she left the lights off and crept over to the window. She would see him outside, looking up. She knew it. She knew all about it.

He wasn't there. She fed her cat in the dark, able to see the cans and the dish by the light of the city coming in the windows. She looked again.

Sean wasn't there.

Rue sat down in the one chair she had, to think that over. Her heart quit hammering; her breathing slowed down. Could she have been mistaken? If she'd been a less-experienced woman she might have persuaded herself that was the case, but Rue had long since made up her mind not to second-guess her instincts. She'd seen Sean. Maybe he wanted to know more about his partner. But he hadn't watched her once she was inside.

Maybe he'd followed her to make sure she was safe, not to spy on her.

It was hard for Rue to pay attention in her History of the British Isles class the next morning. She was still fretting. Should she confront him? Should she stay silent? She'd let her hair go all straggly for class, as she usually did, and she tucked it behind her ear while she bent over her notebook. She was so jangled by her indecision that she let her mind ramble. Her professor caught her by surprise when he asked her what she thought of the policy of the British during the Irish potato famine, and she had a hard time gathering up an answer to give him. To make the day even more unpleasant, while Rue was working on a term paper in the college library, she realized that the brunette across the table was staring at her. Rue recognized that look.

"You're that girl, aren't you?" the girl whispered, after gathering her nerve together.

"What girl?" Rue asked, with a stony face.

"The girl who was a beauty queen? The one who—"

"Do I look like a beauty queen?" Rue asked, her voice sharp and cutting. "Do I look like any kind of queen?"

"Ah, sorry," stammered the girl, her round face flushing red with embarrassment.

"Then shut up," Rue snarled. Rudeness was the most effective defense, she'd found. She'd had to force herself, at first, but as time went on, rudeness had become all too easy. She outstayed the flustered student, too; the girl gathered up her books and pencils and fled the library. Rue had discovered that if she herself left first, it constituted an admission.

After dark, Rue set out to dance rehearsal with anger riding her shoulders.

She debated all the way to Blue Moon. Should she confront her new partner? She needed the job so badly; she liked dancing so much. And though it embarrassed her to admit it to herself, it was a real treat to sometimes look as good as she could, instead of obscuring herself.

Rue reached an internal compromise. If Sean behaved himself during this practice as well as he had during the first, if he didn't start asking personal questions, she would let it go. She could dance this Friday and make some money, if she could just get through the week.

She couldn't prevent the anger rolling around her like a cloud when he came in, but he greeted her quite calmly, and she crammed her rage down to a bearable level.

The dancing went even better that night. She was on edge, and somehow that sharpened her performance. Sean corrected a couple of arm positions, and she carefully complied with his suggestions. She made a few of her own.

If he followed her home, she didn't catch a glimpse of him. She began to relax about the situation.

The next night, he bit her.

"You don't want the first time to be in front of a crowd," he said. "You might scream. You might faint." He seemed quite matter-of-fact about it. "Let's do that thing we were working on, that duet to 'Bolero.'"

"Which is maybe the most hackneyed 'sexy dance' music in the world," she said, willing to pick a fight to cover her anxiety.

"But for a reason," Sean insisted. "Reason" came out "rayson." His Irish accent became more pronounced when he was upset, and Rue enjoyed hearing it. Maybe she would irritate him more often.

The duet they'd been working on was definitely a modern ballet. They started out with Sean approaching Rue, gradually winning her, their hands and the alignment of their bodies showing how much they longed to touch. Finally they entwined in a wonderful complicated meshing of arms and legs, and then Sean lowered her to finish up in the position they'd practiced the night before, leaning Rue back over his arm.

"We'll go very low this time," he said. "My right knee will touch the ground, and your legs should be extended parallel to my left leg. Put your left arm around my neck. Extend your right."

"Can you sustain that? I don't want to end up in a heap on the floor."

"If I brace my right hand on the floor, I can hold us both up." He sounded completely confident.

"You're the vampire," she said, shrugging.

"What's my offense?" He sounded stung.

"I didn't realize you were going to be the boss of us," she said, pleased to have jolted him out of his calm remove. "Aristocrat," Sylvia had called him. Rue knew all about people who thought their money provided them with immunity. She also knew she wasn't being reasonable, but she just couldn't seem to stop being angry.

"You'd like to be the one in charge?" he asked coldly.

"No," she said hastily, "it's just that I—"

"Then what?"

"Nothing! Nothing! Let's do the damn finale!" Every nerve in her body twanged with anxiety.

She got into position with a precision that almost snapped. Her right leg extended slightly in front of her, touching his left leg, which he swept slightly behind him. He took both her hands and clasped them to his chest. His eyes burned into hers. For the first time, his face showed something besides indifference.

*It wasn't smart of me to have a fight with him right before he bites me,* Rue told herself. But the music began. With a feeling of inevitability, Rue moved through the dance with the vampire. Once she moved too far to the right, and once she lost track of her place in the routine, but she recovered quickly both times. And then she was leaning back gracefully, her left arm around Sean's neck, her right arm reaching back, back, her hand in an appealing line. Sean was leaning over her, and she saw his fangs, and she jumped. She couldn't help it.

Then he bit her.

*All her problems were over, her every muscle relaxed, and she was whole again. Her body was smooth and even, and everything inside her was perfect and intact.*

The next thing Rue knew, she was weeping, sitting on the floor with her legs crossed. Sean was sitting by her side, leaning over with his arm around her shoulders.

"It won't be like this again," he said quietly, when he was sure she would understand him.

"Why did that happen? Is it that way for everyone?" She rubbed her face with the handkerchief Sean had handed her. Where he'd kept it, she couldn't imagine.

"No. The first time, you can see what makes you happiest."

*Can,* she noted. She was sure it could also hurt like hell. Sean had been generous.

"It will feel pleasant next time," Sean said. He didn't add, "As long as I want it to," but she could read between the lines. "But it won't be so overwhelming."

She was glad he'd had enough kindness to introduce her to this in private. Of course, she told herself, he hadn't wanted her to collapse on the dance floor, either. She would look stupid then, and so would he. "Can you tell what I'm feeling?" she asked, and she deliberately turned to look him in the eyes.

He met her dark eyes squarely. "Yes, in a muffled way," he said. "I can tell if you are happy, if you are sad—when I bite."

He didn't tell her that now he would always be able to tell how she felt. He didn't tell her that she had tasted sweeter than his memory of honey, sweeter than any human he'd ever bitten.

# CHAPTER THREE

T HEY DANCED TOGETHER for two months before Sean discovered something else about Rue. He wanted to call her "Layla," her real name, but she told him he would forget and call her that in front of someone who…and then she'd shut down her train of thought and asked him to call her Rue like everyone else.

He followed her home every night. Sean wasn't sure if she'd seen him that second night, but he made sure she never saw him again. He was careful. His intention, he told himself, was simply to make sure she arrived at her apartment safely, but he inevitably analyzed what he saw and drew conclusions.

In all those nights, Sean saw her speak to someone only once. Late one Wednesday night, a young man was sitting on the steps of her building. Sean could tell when Rue spotted him. She slowed down perceptibly. By then Sean had bitten her five times, and he could read her so closely that he registered a tiny flinch that would have gone unnoticed by anyone else.

Sean slid through the shadows silently. He maneuvered close enough to be able to help Rue if she needed it.

"Hello, Brandon." Rue didn't sound pleased.

"Hey, Rue. I just thought I might...if you weren't busy... Would you like to go out for a cup of coffee?" He stood up, and now the streetlight showed Sean that the young man was a little older than the common run of students, maybe in his late twenties. He was very thin, but attractive in a solemn way.

Rue stood for a second, her head bowed, as if she were thinking what to do next. The parts of her that Sean had begun to know were brittle and fragile, forged by fear. But now he felt her kindness. She didn't want to hurt this man. But she didn't want to be in his company, either, and Sean was dismayed by how happy this made him.

"Brandon, you're so nice to think of taking me out for coffee," she said gently. "But I thought I made myself real clear last week. I'm not dating right now. I'm just not in that mode."

"A cup of coffee isn't a date."

Her back straightened. Sean considered stepping out of the shadows to stand by her side.

"Brandon, I'm not interested in spending time with you." Her voice was clear and merciless.

The man stared at her in shock. "That's so harsh," he said. He sounded as though he was on the verge of crying. Sean's lip curled.

"I've turned down your invitations three times, Brandon. I've run out of courtesy."

The man pushed past her and walked down the street in such a hurry that he almost knocked over a trash can. Rue swung around to watch him go, her stance belligerent. She might look ruthless to the human eye, but Sean could tell she was full of shame at being so stern with a man as guileless as a persistent puppy. When she went up the steps, Sean drifted down the street, wondering all the while about a beautiful woman who didn't date, a woman who camouflaged what she was under layers of unattractive clothing, a woman who was deliberately rude when her first inclination was to be kind.

Rue May—Layla LaRue LeMay—was hiding. But from what? Or who? He'd been dancing with her for two months now, and he didn't know anything about her.

————◆————

"WE GOT a call from Connie Jaslow," Sylvia said two weeks later. "She wants to hire three couples to dance at a party she's putting on. Since it's warm, she's determined to have a tropical theme."

Rue and Sean, Julie and Thompson, and the third pair of dancers, Megan and Karl, were sitting in the padded folding chairs that Sylvia usually pushed against the walls. For this meeting, they'd pulled the chairs in front of Sylvia's desk.

"She'd like the gals to wear sort of Dorothy Lamour-style outfits, and the guys to wear loincloths and ankle bracelets. She wants some kind of 'native-looking' dance."

"Oh, for God's sake!" said Karl, disgust emphasizing his German accent.

"Connie Jaslow is one of our big repeat customers," Sylvia said. Her eyes went from one to the other of them. "I agree the idea is silly, but Connie pays good money."

"Let's see the costumes," Julie said. Rue had decided Julie was a good-hearted girl, and almost as practical as Sylvia.

"This was what she suggested," Sylvia said. She held up a drawing. The women's costume showed belly button; it was a short flowered skirt, wrapped to look vaguely saronglike, with a matching bra. The long black wig was decorated with artificial flowers.

Rue tried to imagine what she would look like in it, and she thought she'd look pretty good. But then she re-evaluated the low-rider skirt. "It would be that low?" she asked.

"Yes," Sylvia said. "Showing your navel is in right now, and Connie wanted a sort of update to the island look."

"Can't do it," Rue said.

"Something wrong with your button?" teased Thompson.

"My stomach," Rue said, and hoped she could leave it at that.

"I can't believe that. You're as lean as you can be," Sylvia said sharply. She wasn't used to being thwarted.

Rue had a healthy respect for her employer. She knew Sylvia would demand proof. Better to get it over with. Dancers learned to be practical about their bodies. Rue stood abruptly enough to startle Sean, who was leaning against the wall by her chair. Rue pulled up her T-shirt, unzipped her jeans and found she'd worn bikini panties, so she hardly had to push them down. "This would show," Rue said, keeping her voice as level as she could.

The room was silent as the dancers gazed at the thick, jagged scar that ran just to the left of Rue's navel. It descended below the line of the white bikinis.

"Good God, woman!" Karl said. "Was someone trying to gut you?"

"Give me a hysterectomy." Rue pulled her clothes back together.

"We couldn't cover that with makeup," Sylvia said. "Or could we?"

The other two couples and Sylvia discussed Rue's scarred stomach quite matter-of-factly, as a problem to solve.

The debate continued while Rue sat silently, her arms crossed over her chest to hold her agitation in. She became aware that she wasn't hearing a word from Sean. Slowly, she turned to look up at her partner's face. His blue eyes were full of light. He was very angry, livid with rage.

The dispassionate attitudes of the others had made her feel a bit more relaxed, but seeing his rage, Rue began to feel the familiar shame. She wanted to hide from him. And she couldn't understand that, either. Why Sean, whom she knew better than any of the other dancers?

"Rue," Sylvia said, "are you listening?"

"No, sorry, what?"

"Megan and Julie think they can cover it up," Sylvia said. "You're willing to take the job if we can get your belly camouflaged?"

"Sure," she told Sylvia, hardly knowing what she was saying.

"All right, then, two Fridays from now. You all start working on a long dance number right away, faux Polynesian. You'll go on after the jugglers. Julie and Thompson are booked for a party this Saturday night, and Karl and Megan, you're doing a dinner dance at the Cottons' estate on Sunday. Sean, you and Rue are scheduled to open a 'big band' evening at the burn unit benefit."

Rue tried to feel pleased, because she loved dancing to big band music, and she had a wonderful forties dress to wear, but she was still too upset about revealing her scar. What had gotten into her? She'd tried her best to conceal it for years, and all of a sudden, in front of a roomful of relative strangers, she'd pulled down her jeans and shown it to them.

And they'd reacted quite calmly. They hadn't screamed, or thrown up, or asked her what she'd done to deserve that. They hadn't even asked who'd done it to her. To Rue's astonishment, she realized that she was more comfortable with this group of dancers than she was with the other college students. Yet most of those students came from backgrounds that were much more similar to hers than, say, Julie's. Julie had graduated from high school pregnant, had the baby and given it up to the parents of the father. Now she was working nonstop, hoping to gather enough money to buy a small house. If she could do that, she'd told Rue, the older couple would let her have the baby over for the weekends. Megan, a small, intense brunette, was dancing to earn money to get through vet school. She'd seen Rue's stomach and immediately begun thinking how to fix it. No horror, no questions.

The only one who'd reacted with deep emotion had been Sean. Why was he so angry? Her partner felt contempt for her, she decided. Scarred and marred, damaged. If Rue hadn't felt some measure of blame, she could have blown off Sean's reaction, but part of her had always felt guilty that she hadn't recognized trouble, hadn't recognized danger, when it had knocked on her door and asked her out for a date.

That night, when they both left the studio, Sean simply began walking by her side.

"What are you doing?" Rue asked, after giving him a couple of blocks to explain himself. She stopped in her tracks.

"I am going in the same direction you are," he said, his voice calm.

"And how long are you gonna be walking in that direction?"

"Probably as far as your steps will take you."

"Why?"

There it was again, in his eyes, the rage. She shrank back.

"Because I choose to," he said, like a true aristocrat.

"Let me tell you something, buddy," she began, poking him in the chest with her forefinger. "You'll walk me home if I ask you to, or if I let you, not just because you 'choose' to. What will you do if I *choose* not to let you?"

"What will you do," he asked, "if I choose to walk with you, anyway?"

"I could call the police," she said. Being rude wasn't going to work on Sean, apparently.

"Ah, and could the police stop me?"

"Not human cops, maybe, but there are vamps on the force."

"And then you wouldn't have a partner, would you?"

That was a stumper. No, she wouldn't. And since vampires who wanted to dance for a living were scarce, she wouldn't be able to find another partner for a good long while. And that meant she wouldn't be working. And if she wasn't working...

"So you're blackmailing me," she said.

"Call it what you choose," he said. "I am walking you home." His sharp nose rose in the air as he nodded in the right direction.

Frustrated and defeated, Rue shouldered her bag again. He caught the bus with her, and got off with her, and arrived at her building with her, without them exchanging a word the whole way. When Rue went up the steps to the door, he waited until she'd unlocked it and gone inside. He could see her start up the inner stairs, and he retreated to the shadows until he saw a light come on in the second-floor front apartment.

After that, he openly walked her home every night, in silence. On the fourth night, he asked her how her classes were going. She told him about the test she'd had that day in geology. The next night, when he told her to have sweet dreams, he smiled. The M of his mouth turned up at the corners, and his smile made him look like a boy.

On the sixth night, a woman hailed Sean just as he and Rue got off the bus. As the woman crossed the street, Rue recognized Hallie, a Black Moon employee. Rue had met all the Black Moon people, but she did her best to steer clear of them all, both vampire and human. Rue could accept the other Blue Moon dancers as comrades. But the Black Moon performers made her shrink inside herself.

"Hey, what are you two up to?" Hallie said. She was in her late twenties, with curly brown hair and a sweet oval face. It was impossible not to respond to her good cheer; even Sean gave her one of his rare smiles.

"We just left practice," Sean said when Rue stayed silent.

"I just visited my mother," Hallie said. "She seems to be a little better."

Rue knew she had to speak, or she would seem like the most insufferable snob. *Maybe I am a snob*, she thought unhappily. "Is your mom in the hospital?"

"No, she's in Van Diver Home, two blocks down."

Rue had walked past there a couple of times, and thought what a grim place it was, especially for an old folks' home. "I'm sorry," she said.

"She's in the Alzheimer's wing." Hallie's hand was already waving off Rue's expression of sympathy. "If I didn't work for Sylvia, I don't know how I could pay the bills."

"You have another day job, too?"

"Oh, yes. Every day, and nights I don't work for Sylvia, I'm a cocktail waitress. In fact, I'm due back at work. I ran down to see Mom on my break. Good to see both of you."

And off Hallie hurried, her high heels clicking on the pavement. She turned into a bar on the next block, Bissonet's.

Rue and Sean resumed the short walk to Rue's building.

"She's no saint, but it's not as simple as you thought," Sean said when they'd reached her building.

"No, I see that." On an impulse, she gave him a quick hug, then quickly mounted the steps without looking back.

Two weeks later, Blue Moon's three male vampires and three human women were dressing in a remote and barren room in the Jaslow mansion. Connie Jaslow had no consideration for dancers' modesty, since she'd provided one room for both sexes. To an extent, Mrs. Jaslow was correct. Dancers know bodies; bodies were their business, their tools. At least there was an adjacent bathroom, and the women took turns going in to put on their costumes and straighten the black wigs, but the men managed without leaving.

Rick and Phil, the two vampires who ordinarily worked together at "specialty" parties for Black Moon, had polished a juggling act. They would go on first. They were laughing together (Phil only laughed when he was with Rick) as they stood clad only in floral loincloths. "At least we don't have to wear the wigs," the taller Rick said, grinning as he looked over the dancers.

"We look like a bunch of idiots," Julie said bluntly. She tossed her head, and the shoulder-length black wig fell back into place flawlessly.

"At least we're getting paid to look like idiots," Karl said. The driver of the van that had brought them all out to the Jaslow estate, Denny James, came in to tell Karl that the sound system was all set up and ready to go. Denny, a huge burly ex-boxer, worked for Sylvia part-time. Megan and Julie had told Rue that Denny had a closer relationship with Sylvia than employer/ employee, much to Rue's astonishment. The ex-boxer hardly seemed the type to appeal to the sophisticated Sylvia, but maybe that was the attraction.

Anxious about the coming performance, Rue began to stretch. She was already wearing the jungle-print skirt, which draped around to look like a sarong, and matching bikini panties. The bra top matched, too, a wild jungle print over green. The shoulder-length wig swung here and there as she warmed up, and the pink artificial flower wobbled. Rue's stomach was a uniform color, thanks to Julie and Megan.

Karl had brought the CD with their music and given it to the event planner who'd designed the whole party, a weirdly serene little woman named Jeri. On the way into the estate, Rue had noticed that the driveway had been lined with flaming torches on tall poles. The waiters and waitresses were also in costume. Jeri knew how to carry through a theme.

Rue went over the whole routine mentally. Sean came to stand right beside her. On his way out the door with Phil, Rick gave her a kiss on the cheek for luck, and Rue managed to give him a happy smile.

"Nervous?" Sean asked. It came out, "Nairvous?"

"Yes." She didn't mind telling him. *Head up, shoulders square, chest forward, big smile, pretty hands.* "There. I'm okay now."

"Why do you do that? That little...rearrangement?"

"That's what my mother told me to do every time I went on stage, from the time I was five to the time I was twenty."

"You were on stage a lot?"

"Beauty pageants," Rue said slowly, feeling as though she were relating the details of someone else's life. "Talent contests. You name it, I was in it. It cost my parents thousands of dollars a year. I'd win something fairly often, enough to make the effort worth it, at least for my father." She began to sink down in a split. "Press down on my shoulders." His long, thin fingers gripped her and pressed. He always seemed to know how much pressure to apply, though she knew Sean was far stronger than any human.

"Did you have brothers or sisters?" he asked, his voice quiet.

"I have a brother," she said, her eyes closed as she felt her thighs stretch to their limit. She hadn't talked about her family in over a year.

"Is your brother a handsome man?"

"No," Rue said sadly. "No, he isn't. He's a sweet guy, but he's not strong."

"So you didn't win every pageant you entered?" Sean teased, changing the subject.

She opened her eyes and smiled, while rising to her feet very carefully. "I won a few," she said, remembering the glass-fronted case her mother had bought to hold all the trophies and crowns.

"But not all?" Sean widened his eyes to show amazement.

"I came in second sometimes," she conceded, mocking herself, and shot him a sideways look. "And sometimes I was Miss Congeniality."

"You mean the other contestants thought you were the sweetest woman among them?"

"Fooled them, huh?"

Sean smiled at her. "You have your moments." The sweetness of that downturned mouth, when it crooked up in a smile, was incredible.

"You knock my socks off, Sean," she said honestly. She was unable to stop herself from smiling back. He looked very strange in his costume: the flowered loincloth, ankle bracelets made of shells and the short black wig. Thompson was the only one who looked remotely natural in the get-up, and he was gloating about it.

"What does that mean?"

She shook her head, still smiling, and was a little relieved when Denny knocked on the door to indicate that Jeri, the party planner, had signaled that it was time for their appearance. Karl lined the dancers up and looked them over, making a last-minute adjustment here and there. "Stomach looks good," he said briefly, and Rue glanced down. "Julie and Megan did a good job," she admitted. She knew the scar was there, but if she hadn't been looking for it, she would have thought her own stomach was smooth and unmarred.

After Karl's last-minute adjustment of the bright costumes and the black wigs, the six barefoot dancers padded down the carpeted hall to the patio door, and out across the marble terrace into the torch-lit backyard of the Jaslow estate. Rick and Phil loped past them on their way inside, burdened with the things they'd used in their act. "Went great," Rick said. "That backyard's huge."

"It's probably called the garden, not the backyard," Thompson muttered.

Karl said, "Sean, is this the sort of place you grew up in?"

Sean snorted, and Rue couldn't tell if he was deriding his former affluence, or indicating what he'd had had been much better.

Since Rue was shorter than Julie, she was in the middle when the three women stepped out across the marble terrace and onto the grass to begin their routine. Smiling, they posed for the opening bars of the drum music. Julie looked like a different person with the black wig on. Rue had a second to wonder if Julie's own mother would recognize her before the drums began. The routine began with a lot of hulalike hip twitching, the three women gradually rotating in circles. The intense pelvic motion actually felt good. The hand movements were simple, and they'd practiced and practiced doing them in unison. Rue caught a glimpse of Megan turning too fast and hoped the torchlight was obscuring Megan's haste. In her sideways glance, Rue caught a glimpse of a face she'd hoped she'd never see again.

All the years of training she'd had in composure paid off. She kept her smile pasted on her face, she kept up with the dance, and she blanked her mind out. The only thought she permitted herself was a reminder—she'd thought even Julie's family wouldn't recognize her, in the costume and the wig. Neither would her own.

Maybe Carver Hutton IV wouldn't, either.

# CHAPTER FOUR

T HE MUSIC WAS mostly drums, and the beat was fast and demanding. While Megan, Julie and Rue held their positions, the men leaped out, and the crowd gave the expected "Oooooh" at how high the vampires could jump. Sean, Karl and Thompson began their wild dance around the women. It was a good opportunity for her to catch her breath. Without moving her head from its position, she looked over at the spot where she'd seen him standing. Now there was no one there who reminded her of Carver. Maybe it had just been an illusion. Relief swept through her like sweet, cool water through a thirsty throat.

When Sean came to lift her above his head, she gave him a brilliant smile. As he circled, stomping his feet to the beat, she held her pose perfectly, and when he let her fall into his waiting arms, she arched her neck back willingly for the bite. She was ready to feel better, to have that lingering fear erased.

He seemed to sense her eagerness. Before his fangs sank in, she felt his tongue trace a line on her skin, and her arm involuntarily tightened around his neck. As the overwhelming peace flooded her anxious heart, Rue wondered if she was becoming addicted to Sean. "Hi, I'm Rue, and I'm a vampire junkie." She didn't want to become one of those pitiful fangbangers, people who would do almost anything to be bitten.

The audience gave them a round of applause as the women stood up, the men sweeping their arms outward to mark the end of the performance. The crowd goggled curiously at the two dots on the women's necks. Rue stepped forward with Julie and Megan to take her bow, and as she went down she thought she saw Carver Hutton again, out of the corner of her eye. When she straightened, he wasn't there. Was she delusional? She pasted her smile back onto her face.

The six of them ran into the house, waving to the guests as they trotted along, like a happy Polynesian dance troupe that just happened to (almost) all have Caucasian features. They were expected back out on the terrace in party clothes in fifteen minutes. Meanwhile, Denny James would be dismantling their sound system and loading it into the van, because an orchestra was set up to play live music.

When they were scrambling out of the costumes, Rue made her request. "Julie, Megan...do you think you could leave your wigs on?"

The other dancers stopped in the middle of changing and looked at her. Julie had pulled on some thigh-high hose and was buckling the straps of her heels, and Megan had pulled on a sheath dress and gotten her "native" skirt half off underneath it. The male dancers had simply turned their backs and pulled everything off, and now all three were in the process of donning the silk shirts and dress pants they'd agreed on ahead of time. Rick and Phil were helping Denny gather up the costumes and all the other paraphernalia, to store in the van.

But they were all startled by Rue's request. There was a moment of silence.

Julie and Megan consulted with each other in an exchanged glance. "Sure, why not?" Julie said. "Won't look strange. We're all wearing the same outfit. Same wig, why not?"

"But we won't be wearing ours," Karl said, not exactly as if he were objecting, but just pointing out a problem.

"Yeah," Megan said, "but we look cute in ours, and you guys look like dorks in yours."

Karl and Thompson laughed at the justice of that, but Sean was staring at Rue as if he could see her thoughts if he looked hard enough. Phil, who never seemed to talk, was looking at Rue, with worry creasing his face. For the first time, Rue understood that Phil knew who she was. Like the girl in the library, he'd matched her face to the newspaper photos.

The black wig actually looked better with the shining burgundy sheath than Rue's own mahogany hair would have. She would never have picked this color for herself. Megan was wearing a deep green, and Julie, bronze. The men were wearing shirts that matched their partner's dress. Burgundy was not Sean's color, either. They looked at each other and shrugged simultaneously.

Out on the terrace, minutes later, the three couples began dancing to music provided by the live band. After watching for a few minutes, other people began to join them on the smooth marble of the terrace, and the professional couples split up to dance with the guests. This was the part of the job that Rue found most stressful. It was also the most difficult for her partner, she'd noticed. Sean didn't enjoy small talk with companions he hadn't chosen, and he seemed stiff. Thompson was a great favorite with the female guests, always, and Karl was much admired for his sturdy blond good looks and his courtesy, but Sean seemed to both repel and attract a certain class of women, women who were subtly or not so subtly dissatisfied with their lives. They wanted an exotic experience with a mysterious man, and no one did mysterious better than Sean.

John Jaslow, the host, smiled at Rue, and she took his hand and led him to the dance floor. He was a pleasant, balding man, who didn't seem to want anything but a dance.

Men were much easier to please, Rue thought cynically. Most men were happy if you smiled, appeared to enjoy dancing with them, flirted very mildly. Every now and then, she danced with one who was under the impression she was for sale. But she'd met hundreds of men like that while she was going through the pageant circuit, and she was experienced in handling them, though her distaste never ebbed. With a smile and a soothing phrase, she was usually able to divert them and send them away pacified.

Rue and John Jaslow were dancing next to Megan and her partner, who'd introduced himself as Charles Brody. Brody was a big man in his fifties. From the moment he'd taken Megan's hand, he'd been insinuating loudly that he would be delighted if she went to a hotel with him after the party.

"After all, you work for Sylvia Dayton, right?" Brody asked. His hand was stroking Megan's ribs, not resting on them. Rue looked up at her partner anxiously. John Jaslow looked concerned, but he wasn't ready to intervene.

"I work for Blue Moon, not Black Moon," Megan said, quietly but emphatically.

"And you're saying you just go home after one of these affairs, put on your jammies and go to bed by yourself?"

"Mr. Brody, that's exactly what I'm saying," Megan said.

He was quiet for a moment, and Rue and Mr. Jaslow gave each other relieved smiles.

"Then I'll find another woman to dance with, one who'll give a little," Brody said. Abruptly, he let go of Megan, but before he turned to stalk off the terrace, he gave the small dancer a hard shove.

The push was so unexpected, so vicious, that Megan didn't have time to catch herself. She was staggering backward and couldn't catch her balance. Moving faster than she'd thought she was able to move, Rue got behind Megan in time to keep her from hitting the ground.

In a second, Megan was back on her feet, and Mr. Jaslow and Sean were there.

The gasp that had arisen from the few people who'd watched the little episode with Brody gave way to a smattering of applause as Megan and bald Mr. Jaslow glided across the terrace in a graceful swoop.

"Smile," Rue said. Sean had gotten everything right but that. As he two-stepped away with her, his lips were stiff with fury.

"If this were a hundred years ago, I'd kill him," Sean said.

He smiled then, and it wasn't a nice smile. She saw his fangs. She should have been horrified.

She should have been scandalized.

She should have been mortified.

"You're so sweet," she murmured, as she had to a thousand people during her life. This time, she meant it. Though Sean had defused the situation, she had no doubt he would rather have punched Brody, and she liked both reactions.

In five more minutes, their hour was up, and the six dancers eased themselves out of the throng of party guests. Wearily, they folded and bagged the costumes for cleaning and pulled on their street clothes. They were just too tired to be modest. Rue saw a pretty butterfly tattoo on Megan's bottom, and learned that Thompson had an appendectomy scar. But there was nothing salacious about knowing one another like this; they were comrades. Something about this evening had bonded them as no other event ever had.

It had been years since Rue had had friends.

Denny was waiting at the side entrance. The van doors were open, and when Rue scrambled into the back seat, Sean climbed in after her. There was a moment when all the others stared at Sean in surprise, since he always sat in front with Denny, then Megan climbed in after Sean. The middle row was filled with Karl, Julie and Thompson; Rick and Phil clambered in the front with Denny.

It was so pleasant to be sitting down in circumstances that didn't require polite chatter. Rue closed her eyes as the car sped down the long driveway. As they drove back to the city, it seemed a good idea to keep her eyes closed. Now, if she could just prop her head against something...

She woke up when the car came to a stop and the dome light came on. She straightened and yawned. She turned her head to examine her pillow, and found that she'd been sleeping with her head on Sean's shoulder. Megan was smiling at her. "You were out like a light," she said cheerfully.

"Hope I didn't snore," Rue said, trying hard to be nonchalant about the fact that she'd physically intruded on her partner.

"You didn't, but Karl did," Thompson said, easing his way out of the van and stretching once he was on the sidewalk.

"I only breathe loudly," Karl said, and Julie laughed.

"You gotta be the only vampire in the world who takes naps and snores," she said, but to take any sting out of her words, she gave him a hug.

Rue's eyes met Sean's. His were quite unreadable. Though she'd had such a good time with him before they had danced at the Jaslows', he was wearing his usual shuttered look.

"I'm sorry if you were uncomfortable the whole way back," she said. "I didn't realize I was so tired."

"It was fine," he said, and got out, holding out a hand to help her emerge. He unlocked the studio door; Karl and Thompson began unloading the sound system and the dancers set the costumes on a bench outside Sylvia's office. Denny drove off in the empty van.

The small group split up, Megan and Julie getting in the cab they'd called, Karl and Thompson deciding to go to Bissonet's, the bar where Hallie worked. "Why don't you come, Sean?" Karl asked. "You could use some type O."

"No, thanks," Sean said.

"Showing your usual wordy, flowery turn of phrase." Karl was smiling.

"I'll see Rue home," Sean said.

"Always the gentleman," Thompson said, not too fondly. "Sean, sometimes you act like you've got a poker up your ass."

Sean shrugged. He was clearly indifferent to Thompson's opinion.

Thompson's fangs ran halfway out.

Rue and Karl exchanged glances. In that moment, Rue could tell that Karl was worried about a quarrel between the other two vampires, and she took Sean's arm. "I'm ready," she said, and actually gave him a little tug as she started walking north. Sean's good manners required that he set off with her. They took the first two blocks at a good pace, and then turned to stand at the bus stop.

"What frightened you?" he said, so suddenly that she started.

She knew instantly what he was talking about: the seconds at the party when she'd thought she'd seen an all-too-familiar face. But she couldn't believe he'd noticed her fear. She hadn't missed a beat or a step. "How'd you know?" she whispered.

"I know you," he said, with a quiet intensity that centered her attention on him. "I can feel what you feel."

She looked up at him. They were under a streetlight, and she could see him with a stark clarity. Rue struggled inside herself with what she could safely tell him. He was waiting for her to speak, to share her burden with him. Still, she hesitated. She was out of the habit of confiding; but she had to be honest about how safe she felt when she was with Sean, and she could not ignore how much she'd begun to look forward to spending time with him. The relief from fear, from worry, from her sense of being damaged, was like warm sun shining on her face.

He could feel her growing trust; she could see it in his rare smile. The corners of his thin mouth turned up; his eyes warmed.

"Tell me," he said, in a voice less imperative and more coaxing.

What decided her against speaking out was fear for his safety. Sean was strong, and she was beginning to realize he was ruthless where she was concerned, but he was also vulnerable during the daylight hours. Rue followed another impulse; she put her arms around him. She spoke into his chest. "I can't," she said, and she could hear the sadness in her own voice.

His body stiffened under her hands. He was too proud to beg her, she knew, and the rest of the way to Rue's apartment, he was silent.

## CHAPTER FIVE

S HE THOUGHT HE would stalk off, offended, when they reached her place, but, to her surprise, he stuck with her. He held her bag while she unlocked the front door, and he mounted the stairs behind her. While she sure couldn't remember asking him up, Rue didn't tell him to leave, either. She found herself hoping he enjoyed the view all the way up both flights. She tried to remember if she'd made her bed and put away her nightgown that morning.

"Please, come in," Rue said. She knew the new etiquette as well as anyone. Vampires had to be invited into your personal dwelling the first time they visited.

Her cat came running to meet Rue, complaining that her dinner was overdue. The little black-and-white face turned up to Sean in surprise. Then the cat stropped his legs. Rue cast a surreptitious eye over the place. Yes, the bed was neat. She retrieved her green nightgown from the footboard and rolled it into a little bundle, depositing it in a drawer in an unobtrusive way.

"This is Martha," Rue said brightly. "You like cats, I hope?"

"My mother had seven cats, and she named them all, to my father's disgust. She told him they ate the rats in the barn, and so they did, but she'd slip them some milk or some scraps when we had them to spare." He bent to pick up Martha, and the cat sniffed him. The smell of vampire didn't seem to distress the animal. Sean scratched her head, and she began to purr.

The barn? Scraps to spare? That didn't sound too aristocratic. But Rue had no right, she thought unhappily, to question her partner.

"Would you like a drink?" she asked.

Sean was surprised. "Rue, you know I drink..."

"Here," she said, and handed him a bottle of synthetic blood.

She had prepared for his visit, counting on it happening sometime. She had spent some of the little money she had to make him feel welcome.

"Thank you," he said briefly.

"It's room temperature, is that all right? I can heat it in a jiffy."

"It's fine, thanks." He took the bottle from her and opened it, took a sip.

"Where are my manners? Please take off your jacket and sit down." She gestured at the only comfortable chair in the room, an orange velour armchair obviously rescued from a dump. When Sean had taken it (to refuse the chair would have offended her), she sat on a battered folding chair that had come from the same source.

Rue was trying to pick a conversational topic when Sean said, "You have some of the lipstick left on your lower lip."

They'd put on a lot of makeup for the dance, and she thought she'd removed it all before they'd left the Jaslow estate. Rue thought of how silly she must look with a big crimson smudge on her mouth. "Excuse me for a second," she said, and stepped into the tiny bathroom. While she was gone, Sean, moving like lightning, picked up her address book, which he'd spotted lying by the telephone.

He justified this bit of prying quite easily. She wouldn't tell him anything, and he had to know more about her. He wasn't behaving like any aristocrat, that was for sure, but he easily suppressed his guilt over his base behavior.

Flipping through the pages, Sean copied as many numbers as he could on a small piece of notebook paper from Rue's pile of school materials. Several were in one town, Pineville, which had a Tennessee area code. He'd had a vampire friend in Memphis a few years before, and he recognized the number. He'd just replaced the address book when he heard the bathroom door open.

"You're taking the history of my country," Sean said, reading the spines of the textbooks piled on the tiny table that served as Rue's desk.

"It's the history of all the British Isles," she said, trying not to grin. "But yes, I am. It's an interesting course."

"What year have you reached in your course of study?"

"We're talking about Michael Collins."

"I knew him."

"What?" Her mouth fell open, and she knew she must look like an idiot. For the first time, she realized the weight of the years on Sean's shoulders, the knowledge of history and people that filled his head. "You knew him?"

Sean nodded. "A fiery man, but not to my taste."

"Could—would—you talk to my class about your recollections?"

Sean looked dismayed. "Oh, Rue, it was so long ago. And I'm not much of a crowd pleaser."

"That's not true," she said, adding silently, *You please me.* "Think about it? My professor would be thrilled. She's a nut about everything Irish."

"Oh, and where's she from?"

"Oklahoma."

"A far way from Ireland."

"You want another drink?"

"No." He looked down at the bottle, seemed surprised he'd drained it. "I must be going, so you can get a little sleep. Do you have classes tomorrow?"

"No, it's Saturday. I get to sleep in."

"Me, too."

Sean had actually made a little joke, and Rue laughed.

"So do you sleep in a regular bed?" she asked. "Or a coffin, or what?"

"In my own apartment I have a regular bed, since the room's light-tight. I have a couple of places in the city where I can stay, if my apartment's too far away when it gets close to dawn. Like hostels for vampires. There are coffins to sleep in, at those places. More convenient."

Rue and Sean stood. She took the empty bottle from him and leaned backward to put it by her sink. Suddenly the silence became significant, and her pulse speeded up.

"Now I'll kiss you good-night," Sean said deliberately. In one step he was directly in front of her, his hand behind her head, his spread fingers holding her in exactly the right position. Then his mouth was on Rue's, and after a moment, during which Rue held very still, his tongue touched the seam of her lips. She parted them.

There was the oddity of Sean's mouth being cool; and the oddity of kissing Sean, period. She was finally sure that Sean's interest in her was that of a man for a woman. For a cool man, he gave a passionate kiss.

"Sean," she whispered, pulling back a little.

"What?" His voice was equally as quiet.

"We shouldn't..."

"Layla."

His use of her real name intoxicated her, and when he kissed her again, she felt only excitement. She felt more comfortable with the vampire than she'd felt with any man. But the jolt she felt, low down, when his tongue touched hers, was not what she'd call comfortable. She slid her arms around his neck and abandoned herself to the kiss. When Rue felt his body pressing against her, she knew he found their contact equally exciting.

His mouth traveled down her neck. He licked the spot where he usually bit her. Her body flexed against his, involuntarily.

"Layla," he said, against her ear, "who did you see that frightened you so much?"

It was like a bucket of cold water tossed in her face. Everything in her shut down. She shoved him away from her violently. "You did this to satisfy your curiosity? You thought if you softened me up, I'd answer all your questions?"

"Oh, of course," he said, and his voice was cold with anger. "This is my interrogation technique."

She lowered her face into her hands just to gain a second of privacy.

She was half inclined to take him literally. He was acting as if she was the unreasonable one, as if all the details of her short life should belong to him.

There was a knock on the door.

Their eyes met, hers wide with surprise, his questioning. She shook her head. She wasn't expecting anyone.

Rue went to the door slowly and looked through the peephole. Sean was right behind her, moving as silently as only vampires could move, when she unlocked the door and swung it open.

Thompson stood there, and Hallie. Between the two, awkwardly, they supported Hallie's partner, David. David was bleeding profusely from his left thigh. His khakis were soaked with blood. The vampire's large dark eyes were open, but fluttering.

Thompson's gaze was fixed on Rue; when he realized that Sean was standing behind her, he was visibly startled.

"Oh, come in, bring him in!" Rue exclaimed, shocked. "What happened?" She spared a second to be glad none of her neighbors seemed to be up. She shut the door before any of them roused.

Hallie was sobbing. Her tears had smeared her heavy eye makeup. "It was because of me," she sobbed. "Thompson and Karl came in the bar. David was already there, he'd been having words with this jerk…" While she was trying to tell Rue, she was helping David over to Rue's bed. Thompson was not being quite as much assistance as he should have been.

Sean whipped a towel from the rack in the bathroom and spread it on Rue's bed before the two eased the wounded David down. Hallie knelt and swung David's legs up, and David moaned.

"It was the Fellowship," Thompson said as Hallie unbuckled David's belt and began to pull his sodden slacks down.

The Fellowship of the Sun was to vampires as the Klan was to African Americans. The Fellowship purported to be a civic organization, but it functioned more like a church, a church that taught its adherents the religion of violence.

"The other night I turned down this guy in the bar," Hallie said. "He just gave me the creeps. Then he found out I worked for Black Moon, and that I performed with David, you know, for the show, and he was waiting for me tonight..."

"Take it easy," Rue said soothingly. "You're gonna hyper-ventilate, Hallie. Listen, you go wash your face, and you get a bottle of TrueBlood for David, because he needs some blood. He's gonna heal."

Snuffling, Hallie ducked into the bathroom.

"He decided to get Hallie tonight, and David intervened?" Sean asked Thompson quietly. Rue listened with one ear while she stanched the bleeding by applying pressure with a clean kitchen towel. It rapidly reddened. She was not as calm as she'd sounded. In fact, her hands were shaking.

"David likes her, and she's his partner," Thompson said, as if David's intervention required an excuse. "Karl had left earlier, and David and I came out just in time to catch the show. The bastard had his arm wrapped around Hallie's neck. But he dropped her and went for David real fast, with a knife."

"Out on the street, or in the bar?"

"Behind the bar, in the alley."

"Where's the body?"

Rue stiffened. Her hands slipped for a moment, and the bleeding began again. She pressed harder.

"I took him over the rooftops and deposited him in an alley three blocks away. David didn't bite him. He just hit him—once."

Rue knew no one was thinking of calling the police. And she was all too aware that justice wasn't likely to be attainable.

"He'll heal faster if he has real blood, right?" she said over her shoulder. She hesitated. "Shall I give him some?" She tried to keep her voice even. She had hardly exchanged ten words with David, who was very brawny and very tall. He had long, rippling black hair and a gold hoop in one ear. She knew, through Megan and Julie, that David was often booked to strip at bridal showers, as well as performing with Hallie in private clubs. In her other life, Rue would have walked a block to avoid David. Now she was pulling up the sleeve of her sweater to bare her wrist.

"No," said Sean very definitely. He pulled the sleeve right back down, and she stared at him, her mouth compressed with irritation. She might have felt a smidgen of relief, but Sean had no right to dictate to her.

Hallie had emerged from the bathroom, looking much fresher. "Let Sean give blood, Rue," she said, reading Rue's face correctly. "It won't make him weak, like it would you. If Sean won't, I will."

David, who'd been following the conversation at least a little, said, "No, Hallie. I have bitten you already three times this week." David had a heavy accent, perhaps Israeli.

Without further ado, Sean knelt by the bed and held his wrist in front of David. David took Sean's arm in both his hands and bit. A slight flexing of Sean's lips was the only sign that he'd felt the fangs. They all watched as David's mouth moved against Sean's wrist.

"Sean, what a dark horse you are, me boyo, visiting the lady here after hours." Thompson's attempt at an Irish accent was regrettable. His eyes lit on the empty TrueBlood bottle by the sink. "And her all ready for your arrival."

"Oh, shut up, Thompson." Rue was too tired to think of being polite. "As soon as Sean finishes his, ah, donation, all of you can leave, except David. He can rest here for a while until he feels well enough to go."

After a few minutes, David put Sean's arm away from him, and Sean rolled his own sleeve over his wrist. Moving rather carefully, Sean picked up his jacket, carefully draped it over his arm.

"Good night, darlin'," he said, giving her a quick kiss on the cheek. "Kick David out after a couple of hours. He'll be well enough by then."

"I'll stay," Hallie said. "He got hurt on account of me, after all."

Sean looked relieved. Thompson looked disgruntled. "I'll be shoving off, then," he said. Hallie thanked him very nicely for helping her with David, and he was unexpectedly gracious about waving her gratitude away.

"We'll practice Sunday night," Sean said to Rue, his hand on the doorknob. "Can you be there at eight?" He'd been making plans for Saturday night while David had been taking blood from his wrist.

"I forgot to tell you," Thompson said. "Sylvia left a message on my cell. We have a company meeting Sunday night, at seven." It would just be dark at seven, so the vampires could attend.

"I'll see you there, Rue," Sean said. "And we can practice, after."

"All right," Rue said, after a marked pause.

Thompson said, "Good night, Rue, Hallie. Feel better, David."

"Good night, all," she said, and shut the door on both of them. She had one more bottle of synthetic blood, which she gave to David. She sat down in the chair while Hallie perched on the bed with David as he drank it. She tried valiantly to stay awake, but when she opened her eyes, she found two hours had passed, and her bed was empty. The bloody towels had been put to soak in the bathtub in cold water, and the empty bottles were in the trash.

Rue was relieved. "You and me, Martha," she said to the cat, who'd come out of hiding now that the strangers were gone. Rue's bed looked better than anything in the world, narrow and lumpy as it was. In short order, she'd cleaned her face and teeth and pulled on her pajamas. Martha leaped onto the bed and claimed her territory, and Rue negotiated with her so she'd have room for her own legs.

Rue was really tired, but she was also shaken. After all, there was a human dead on the street. She waited to feel a wave of guilt that never hit shore. Rue knew that if Hallie had been by herself, it would be Hallie lying bleeding on the street.

*Been there, done that*, Rue told herself coldly. *And all I got were the lousy scars to prove it.*

As for the shock she'd gotten at the Jaslows', a glimpse of the face she feared above all others, she was now inclined to think she'd imagined it. He would have made sure she noticed him, if he'd known she was there. He would have come after her again.

He'd sworn he would.

But it was funny that tonight, of all nights, she'd thought she'd seen him. At first, she'd imagined him everywhere, no matter how many times she'd called the police station to make sure he was still in the hospital. Maybe, once again, it was time to give Will Kryder a call again.

She imagined Sean lying in a coffin and smiled, just a curve of the lips before she drifted off to sleep.

Actually, Sean was on the road.

———◆———

SEAN HAD a feeling he was doing something wrong, going behind Rue's—Layla's—back like this, but he was determined to do it anyway. If he'd asked Thompson to help, he had no doubt the younger vampire could have tracked down any information Sean needed on the damned computer. But Sean had never gotten used to the machines; it might take him twenty more years to accept them.

Like cars. Cars had been tough, too. Sean hadn't learned to drive until the sixties. He had loved phonographs from their inception, though, because they'd provided music for dancing, and he had bought a CD player as soon as he could. Words were hard for Sean, so dancing had always been his means of expression, from the time he'd become free to dance.

So here he was, off to collect information the old-fashioned way. He would get to Pineville tonight, find a place to hole up until he woke the next night, and then get his investigation under way.

Sean knew Rue had a fear that ran so deep she couldn't speak of it. And once he'd decided Rue was his business, it had become his job to discover what she feared. He had done some changing through the centuries, but the way he'd grown up had ingrained in him the conviction that if a man claimed a woman as his family—or his mate—he had to protect her.

And how could he protect her if he didn't understand the threat?

While Rue rose late to have a leisurely breakfast, clean her apartment and wash her clothes, Sean, who had consulted his housing directory, was sleeping in the vampire room of the only motel large enough to boast one, right off the interstate at the exit before Pineville. He had a feeling it was the first time the clerk had rented the room to an actual vampire. He'd heard that human couples sometimes took the room for some kinky play-acting. He found that distasteful. The room—windowless, with two aligned doors, both with heavy locks, and a black velour curtain in between—had two coffins sitting side by side on the floor. There was a small refrigerator in the corner, with several bottles of synthetic blood inside. There was a minimalist bathroom. At least the coffins were new, and the padding inside was soft. Sean had paid an exorbitant amount for this Spartan accommodation, and he sighed as he undressed and climbed into the larger of the two coffins. Before he lay down, he looked over at the inner door to make sure all its locks were employed. He pulled the lid down, seconds before he could feel the sun come up.

Then he died.

# CHAPTER SIX

W HEN SEAN FELT life flowing back into his body that night, he was very hungry. He woke with his fangs out, ready to sink into some soft neck. But it was rare that Sean indulged himself in fresh human blood; these days, the sips he took from Rue were all he wanted. He pulled the synthetic blood from the refrigerator, and since he didn't like it cold, he ran hot water in the bathroom and set the bottle in the sink while he showered. He hated to wash the scent of Rue from his skin, but he wanted to seem as normal as possible to the people he talked to tonight. The more humanlike a vampire could look and act, the more likely humans were to be open to conversation. Sean had noticed that interactions were easier for Thompson, who still had clear memories of what it was like to breathe and eat.

He'd written down the numbers and names from Rue's book, just in case his memory played tricks with him. One of the numbers was self-explanatory—"Mom and Dad," she'd written by it. "Les," she'd written by another, and that was surely one he would have to explore; a single man might be a rival. The most interesting numbers were by the notation "Sergeant Kryder." She'd labeled one number "police station" and the second number "home."

Pineville looked like almost any small town. It seemed to be dominated by one big business—Hutton Furniture Manufacturing, a huge plant that ran around the clock, Sean noted. The sign in front of the library read Camille Hutton Library, and the largest church complex boasted a whole building labeled Carver Hutton II Family Life Center.

The tire company was owned by a Hutton, and one of the car dealerships, too.

There was no sign crediting the Huttons with owning the police force, but Sean suspected that might be close to the truth. He found the station easily; it was right off the town square, a low redbrick building. The sidewalk from the parking area to the front door was lined with azaleas just about to bloom. Sean opened the swinging glass door to see a young policeman with his feet up on the counter that divided the public and private parts of the front room. A young woman in civilian clothes—short and tight civilian clothes—was using a copier placed against the wall to the left, and the two were chatting as Sean came in.

"Yes, sir?" said the officer, swinging his feet to the floor.

The young woman glanced at Sean, then did a double take. "Vampire," she said in a choked voice.

The man glanced from her to Sean in a puzzled way. Then he seemed to take in Sean's white face for the first time, and he visibly braced his shoulders.

"What can I do to help you, sir?" he asked.

"I want to speak with Sergeant Kryder," Sean said, smiling with closed lips.

"Oh, he retired," called the girl before the young man could answer. The man's name tag read "Farrington." He wasn't pleased at the girl's homing in on his conversation with the vampire.

"Where might I find him?" Sean asked.

Officer Farrington shot a quelling glance at the girl and pulled a pencil out of his drawer to draw Sean a map. "You take a left at the next stop sign," he told Sean. "Then go right two blocks, and it's the white house on the corner with the dark green shutters."

"Might be gone," said the girl sulkily.

"Barbara, you know they ain't left yet."

"Packing up, I heard."

"Ain't left yet." Farrington turned to Sean. "The Kryders are moving to their place in Florida."

"I guess it was time for him to retire," Sean said gently, willing to learn what he could.

"He took it early," the girl said. "He got all upset about the Layla LeMay thing."

"Barbara, shut up," Officer Farrington said, his voice very sharp and very clear.

Sean tried hard to look indifferent. He said, "Thank you very much," and left with the instructions, wondering if they'd call ahead to the ex-sergeant, warn him of Sean's impending visit.

———◆———

SERGEANT KRYDER had indeed gotten a call from the police station. His front light was on when Sean parked in front of his modest house. Sean didn't have a plan for interrogating the retired policeman. He would play it by ear. If Rue had written the man's phone number in her book, then the man had befriended her.

Sean knocked at the door very gently, and a slim, clean-shaven man of medium height with thinning fair hair and a guarded smile opened the door. "Can I help you?" the man asked.

"Sergeant Kryder?"

"Yes, I'm Will Kryder."

"I would like to speak with you about a mutual friend."

"I have a mutual friend with a vampire?" Kryder seemed to catch himself. "Excuse me, I didn't mean to offend. Please come in." The older man didn't seem sure about the wisdom of inviting Sean in, but he stood aside, and Sean stepped into the small living room. Cartons were stacked everywhere, and the house looked bare. The furniture was still there, but the walls were blank, and none of the normal odds and ends were on the tables.

A dark-haired woman was standing in the doorway to the kitchen, a dish towel in her hand. Two cats rubbed her ankles, and a little Pekingese leaped from the couch, barking ferociously. He stopped when he got close to Sean. He backed up, whining. The woman actually looked embarrassed.

"Don't worry," Sean said. "You can never tell with dogs. Cats generally like us." He knelt and held out a hand, and the cats both sniffed it without fear. The Pekingese retreated into the kitchen.

Sean stood, and the woman extended her hand. She had an air of health and intelligence about her that was very appealing. She looked Sean in the eyes, apparently not knowing that he could do all kinds of things with such a direct look. "I'm Judith," she said. "I apologize for the appearance of the house, but we're leaving in two days. When Will retired, we decided to move down to our Florida house. It's been in Will's family for years."

Will had been watching Sean intently. "Please have a seat," he said.

Sean sank into the armchair, and Will Kryder sat on the couch. Judith said, "I'll just go dry the dishes," and vanished into the kitchen, but Sean was aware that she could hear them if she chose.

"Our mutual friend?" Will prompted.

"Layla."

Will's face hardened. "Who are you? Who sent you here?"

"I came here because I want to find out what happened to her."

"Why?"

"Because she's scared of something. Because I can't make it go away unless I know what it is."

"Seems to me if she wanted you to know, she would tell you herself."

"She is too frightened."

"Are you here to ask me where she is?"

Sean was surprised. "No. I know where she is. I see her every night."

"I don't believe you. I think you're some kind of private detective. We knew someone would be coming sooner or later, someone like you. That's why we're leaving town. If you think you can get rid of us easy, let me tell you, you can't." Will's pleasant face was set in firm lines. He suddenly had a gun in his lap, and it was pointed at Sean.

"It's easy to see you haven't met a vampire before," Sean said.

"Why is that?"

Before Will could pull the trigger, Sean had the gun. He bent the barrel and tossed it behind him.

"Judith!" Will yelled. "Run!" He dove for Sean, apparently intending to grapple with Sean until Judith could get clear.

Sean held the man still by clamping Kryder's hands to his sides. He said, "Calm yourself, Mr. Kryder." Judith was in the room now, a butcher knife in her hands. She danced back and forth, reluctant to stab Sean but determined to help her husband.

Sean liked the Kryders.

"Please be calm, both of you," he said, and the quiet of his voice, the stillness of his posture, seemed to strike both of the Kryders at the same time. Will stopped struggling and looked at Sean's white face intently. Judith lowered the knife, and Sean could tell she was relieved to be able to.

"She calls herself Rue May now," he told them. "She's going to the university, and she has a cat named Martha."

Judith's eyes widened. "He does know her," she said.

"He could have found that out from surveillance." Will was not so sure.

"How did you meet her?" Judith asked.

"I dance with her. We dance for money."

The couple exchanged a glance.

"What does she do before she goes on stage?" Judith asked suddenly.

"Head up, chest out, shoulders square, big smile, pretty hands." Sean smiled his rare smile.

Will Kryder nodded at Judith. "I reckon you can let go of me now," he told Sean. "How is she?"

"She's lonely. And she saw something the other night that scared her."

"What do you know about her?"

"I know she was a beauty queen. I know she danced in a lot of contests. I know she never seems to hear from her family. I know she has a brother. I know she's hiding under another name."

"Have you seen her stomach?"

"The scars, yes."

"You know how she got that way?" Kryder didn't seem to be concerned with how Sean had come to see the scars.

Sean shook his head.

"Judith, you tell him."

Judith sat on the couch beside her husband. Her hands clasped tightly in her lap, she appeared to be organizing her thoughts.

"I taught her when she was in tenth grade," Judith said. "She'd won a lot of titles even then. Layla is just...beautiful. And her mother pushed and pushed. Her mother is an ex-beauty queen, and she married Tex LeMay after she'd had two years of college, I think. Tex was a handsome man, still is, but he's not tough, not at all. He let LeeAnne push him around at home, and at work he let his boss stomp on what was left of his...manhood."

Sean didn't have to feign his interest. "His boss?"

"Carver Hutton III." Will's face was rigid with dislike as he spoke the name.

"The family that owns this town."

"Yes," Judith said. "The family that owns this town. That's who Tex works for. The other LeMay kid, Les, was always a dim bulb compared to Layla. Les is a good boy, and I think he's kept in touch with Layla—did you say she calls herself Rue these days? Les is off at college now, and he doesn't come home much."

"Carver IV came back from his last year of college one Christmas, two years ago," Will said. "Layla'd been elected Christmas Parade Queen, and she was riding in the big sleigh—'course, it's really a horse-drawn wagon, we don't get snow every year—and she was wearing white, and a sparkly crown. She looked like she was born to do that."

"She's a sweet girl, too," Judith said unexpectedly. "I'm not saying she's an angel or a saint, but Layla's a kind young woman. And she's got a backbone like her mother. No, I take that back. Her mother's got a strong will, but her backbone doesn't even belong to her. It belongs to the Social God."

Will laughed, a small, choked laugh, as if the familiar reference sparked a familiar response. "That's the god that rules some small towns," he said to Sean. "The one that says you have to do everything exactly correct, follow all the rules, and you'll go to heaven. Social heaven."

"Where you get invited to all the right places and hang around with all the right people," Judith elaborated.

Sean was beginning to have a buzzing feeling in his head. He recognized it as intense anger.

"What happened?" he asked. He was pretty sure he knew.

"Carver asked Layla out. She was only seventeen. She was flattered, excited. He treated her real well the first two times, she told me. The third time, he raped her."

"She came over here," Judith said. "Her mom wouldn't listen, and her dad said she must be mistaken. He asked her didn't she wear a lot of perfume and makeup, or a sexy dress." Judith shook her head. "She'd—it was her first time. She was a mess. Will called the chief of police at the time. He wasn't a monster," Judith said softly. "But he wasn't willing to lose his job over arresting Carver."

"She shut herself in the house and wouldn't come out for two weeks," Will said. "Her mother called us, told us to quit telling lies about the Huttons. She said Layla had just misunderstood the situation. Her exact words."

"Then," said Judith heavily, "Layla found out she was pregnant."

The buzzing in Sean's head grew louder, more insistent. He had never felt like this before, in his hundreds of years.

"She called Carver and told him. I guess she thought something so serious would bring him to his senses. Maybe she imagined that his parents had brought on all his violence. Maybe she thought he would do right by her somehow. She was just seventeen. I don't know what she thought. Maybe she wanted him to take her to a doctor, I don't know. She didn't want to tell her parents."

"He decided to take care of it himself," Sean said.

"Yeah," Will said. "He lost his mind. Usually, he can act like a real person when other people are around." Will Kryder sounded as detached as if he were discussing the habits of an exotic animal, but his hands were clasped in front of him so tightly that they were white. "Carver couldn't maintain the facade that night. He pulled up in front of the LeMays' house, and Layla came out, without saying anything to Tex or LeeAnne about where she was going. But Les was watching out the window, and he saw…he saw…"

"After he socked her in the face a few times, he broke his soda bottle and used that," Judith said simply. There was a long moment of silence. "Les got him off in time to save Layla's life, by hitting Carver with his baseball bat…he was on the high school team, then."

"Go on," Sean managed to say. They'd been lost in these tragic memories, but when they heard his voice, they looked up, to be absolutely terrified by Sean's face. "I'm not angry with you," Sean said, very quietly. "Go on."

"The scene at the hospital was—you can imagine," Will said, his voice weary. "She lost the baby, of course, and there was considerable damage. Permanent damage. She was in the hospital for a while."

"No one could ignore *that*," Judith said bitterly. "But the Huttons got a good lawyer, of course, and he made a case for insanity. Here in Pineville, of course, a Hutton won't get convicted of jaywalking. He was declared temporarily insane, and the judge sentenced him to time in a mental institution and ordered his family to pay all Layla's medical expenses. He did grant Layla a restraining order against Carver ever contacting her again, or even coming within a hundred feet of her. I guess that's worth the paper it's printed on. When the mental doctors decided Carver was 'stabilized,' he could be released, and he had to go through so many courses of outpatient anger management and other therapy. That took four years." She shook her head. "Of course, that doesn't mean jack."

"He mutilates Layla, he causes the death of his own child in her womb, and after a token sentence, he walks free." Sean shook his head, his expression remote. "Since I've lived in America, I've admired its justice system. So much better than when I was a boy in Ireland, when children could be hung for stealing bread when they were hungry. But this isn't any better."

The Kryders both looked embarrassed, as if they were personally responsible for the injustice. "That's another reason we're moving," Will said. "Sooner or later, when we least expect it, Carver III will make us pay for backing Layla up. She stayed with us some, when she was convalescing. She didn't want to see her parents. Les used to come over, visit her. Not LeeAnne. Not Tex."

Sean didn't express incredulity, and he didn't comment on Layla's family's behavior. He'd seen worse in his long life, but he hadn't seen worse done to someone he cared about as much as he cared about Layla LaRue LeMay.

"Does she call you?" Sean asked.

"Yes, she does, from time to time. She'll call here, or she'll call the station to talk to Will, to find out if Carver's out yet."

"And is he?"

"Yes. After four years, he's off all supervision now. He's footloose and fancy-free."

"And is he living here?"

"No. He left town right away."

"She saw him," Sean said out loud.

"Oh, no. Where?"

"At a party, where we were dancing."

"Did he approach her?"

"No."

"Did he see her?" Judith had hit the nail on the head.

Sean said slowly, "I don't know." Then he said, "But I have to get back. Now."

Will said, "I hope you're planning on being good to her. If I hear different, I'll come back and track you down with a stake in my hand. She's had enough trouble."

Sean stood and bowed, in a very old-fashioned way. "We'll see you in Florida," he said.

He left Pineville, pushing the rental car to its limit, so he could make the last plane that would get him into the city in time to find a daytime resting place. There was a safe apartment very close to the airport, maintained by the vampire hierarchy. He called ahead to reserve a coffin, and got on the plane after making sure there was an emergency space in the tail where he could wait if sunlight caught them. But all went well, and he was in a room with three other occupied coffins by the time the sun came up.

# CHAPTER SEVEN

THE PERSONNEL OF Blue Moon Entertainment and Black Moon Productions were draped around the big practice room in various positions of weariness. It was a scant hour after darkness had fallen, and some of the vampires looked sluggish. Every one of them clutched a bottle of synthetic blood. Most of the humans had coffee mugs.

Rue had come in full disguise. The more she'd thought about the glimpse she'd had of the man who'd looked so much like Carver Hutton IV, the more spooked she'd gotten. Between that fear and her upsetting spat with Sean, and the remembered tingle she'd felt when they kissed, she hadn't been worth anything during the weekend so far. She'd performed her regular weekend chores, but in a slapdash fashion. She hadn't been able to study at all.

When Sean came in, wearing sweatpants and a Grateful Dead T-shirt, her pulse speeded up in a significant way. He folded to the floor by her, his back against the glass of the mirror as hers was, and scooted closer until their shoulders and hips touched.

Sean was silent, and she was too self-conscious to look up at his eyes. She'd half expected to hear from him the night before, and when the phone hadn't rung and there'd been no knock at her door, she'd felt quite disconcerted. Men had seldom walked away from her, no matter how rocky their relationship had grown. *I am not going to ask him where he's been*, she swore to herself.

Sylvia was talking on the phone and smoking, which all the human dancers detested. She was doing it to prove she was the boss. Rue made a face and tried to arrange herself so her back was comfortable. The wall wasn't friendly to her spine, which had been jolted when she caught Megan after Charles Brody had shoved her. Megan was moving a little stiffly. Hallie looked subdued and David seemed healed, as far as Rue could tell. She hoped this week would be a better one for the entertainment troupe as a whole.

Rue sighed and tried to shift her weight slightly to her right hip. To her astonishment, in the next moment she felt herself being lifted. Sean had spread his legs, and he put her down between them, so her back rested against his stomach and chest. He scooted his butt out from the wall to give her a little incline. She was instantly more comfortable.

Rue figured if she didn't make any big deal out of it, no one else would either, so she didn't say a word or betray the surprise she felt. But she relaxed against Sean, knowing he would interpret that signal correctly as a thank-you.

Sylvia hung up at last. A black-haired female vampire with beautiful clear skin and dead eyes said, "Sylvia, we all know you're top dog. Put out the damn cigarette." The vampire waved her elegant hand at Sylvia imperiously.

"Abilene, tell me how you and Mustafa are doing," Sylvia said, blowing out smoke, but then she stubbed out the cigarette.

A tall human with a full mustache, Mustafa had more muscles than any man needed, in Rue's opinion. He was very dark complexioned, and a slow thinker. Rue wondered about the dynamics of this team, since the vampire half was a woman. How did that work? Did she do the lifts? Belatedly, Rue realized that in Black Moon's form of entertainment, lifting was probably irrelevant.

"We're doing fine," Abilene said. "You got any comments, Moose?" That was her pet name for her giant partner, but no one else dared use it.

"The pale woman," he said, his voice heavily accented and deep as a foghorn. Moose seemed to be a man of few words.

"Oh, yeah, the last gig we did, the party for the senator," Abilene said. "The wife of one of the, ah, legislators... I don't know how she got there, why her husband brought her, but she turned out to be Fellowship."

"Were you hurt?" Sylvia asked.

"She had a knife," Abilene said. "Moose was on top of me, so it was an awkward moment. You sure I can't kill the customers?" Abilene smiled, and it wasn't a nice smile.

"No, indeed," Sylvia said briskly. "Haskell take care of it?"

For the first time, Rue noticed the sleek man leaning against the wall by the door. She seldom had dealings with Haskell, since the Black Moon people needed more protection than the Blue

Moon dancers. Haskell was a vampire, with smooth, short blond hair and glacier-blue eyes. He had the musculature of a gymnast, and the wary, alert attitude of a bodyguard.

"I held her until her husband and his flunky could get her out of there," Haskell said quietly.

"Her name?"

"Iris Lowry."

Sylvia made a note of the name. "Okay, we'll watch for her. I may have my lawyer write Senator Lowry a letter. Hallie? David?"

"We're fine," David said briskly. Rue looked down at her hands. No reason to relate the incident, even though it had ended with a death...a death that hadn't even made the papers.

"Rick? Phil?" The two men glanced at each other before answering.

"The last group we entertained, at the Happy Horseman—it was an S&M group, and we gave them a good show."

They weren't talking about juggling. Rue tried to keep her face blank. She didn't want her distaste to show. These people had shown her nothing but courtesy and comradeship.

"They wanted me to leave Phil there when our time was up," Rick said. "It was touch-and-go for a few minutes." The two vampires were always together, but they were very different. Rick was tall and handsome in a bland, brown-on-brown kind of way. Phil was small and slim, delicate. In fact, Rue decided, she might have mistaken him for a fourteen-year-old. *Maybe when he died he was that young*, she thought, and felt a pang of pity. Then Phil happened to look at Rue, and after meeting his pale, bottomless eyes, she shivered.

"Oh, no," said Sylvia, and Phil turned to his employer. "Phil?" Her voice became gentle. "You know we're not going to let anyone else touch you, unless you want that to happen. But remember, you can't attack someone just because they want you. You're so gorgeous, people are always going to want you."

Sylvia braced herself in the face of that continued, terrifying gaze. "You know the deal, Phil," Sylvia said more firmly. "You have to leave the customers alone." After a long, tense pause, Phil nodded, almost imperceptibly.

"So, you think we need another minder, like Haskell? For nights when we're double-booked on Black Moon shows?" Sylvia asked the group. "Denny's a great guy, but he's really just a lifting-and-setup kind of fellow. He's not aggressive enough to be a minder, and he's human."

"Wouldn't hurt to have someone else," Rick said. "It would've taken some of the strain off if there'd been a third party there. It looked like it was going to be me against all of them for a little while. I hate to injure the client base, but I thought I might have to. People who like that kind of show are ready for a little violence, anyway."

Sylvia nodded, made another note. "What about you Blue Moon people?" she asked, obviously not expecting any response. "Oh, Rue. Only a couple of the Black Mooners have seen you in your dancing clothes. Take off the other stuff, so they can see what you really look like. I'm not sure they could recognize you in a crowd."

Rue hadn't planned on becoming the center of attention, but there was no point of making a production of this request.

She stood and unbuttoned the flannel shirt, pulled off the glasses and stepped out of the old corduroy pants she'd pulled on to cover her practice clothes. She held out her arms, inviting them to study her in her T-shirt and shorts, and then she sank down to the floor again. Sean's arms crossed over her and pulled her tightly against him. This was body language anyone could understand—"Mine!" The Black Moon people almost all smiled—Phil and Mustafa being the exceptions—and nodded, both to acknowledge Rue and to say they'd noted Sean's possessiveness.

Rue wanted to whack Sean across his narrow aristocratic face.

She also wanted to kiss him again.

But there was one thing she had to say. "We had some trouble," she said hesitantly. She could understand David and Hallie's silence. They hadn't been on a professional engagement—*and* a man had died. But she couldn't understand why Megan wasn't speaking out.

Sylvia said, "With whom?" Her eyebrows were raised in astonishment.

"Guy named Charles Brody. He got mad when Megan wouldn't take money to meet him afterward. He mentioned your name, Sylvia, but he wouldn't...he didn't accept it too well when we told him we didn't work for Black Moon. He acted like it was going to be okay, that he accepted Megan's refusal, but when he turned to leave, he shoved her down."

"I don't recognize the name, but he could've hired us before," Sylvia said. "Thanks, I'll put him in the watch-for file. Were you hurt?" She waited impatiently for Megan's reply.

"No," Megan said. "Rue caught me. I would've said something, but I'd pretty much forgotten it." She shrugged. She clearly wasn't too pleased with Rue for bringing up the incident.

"I want to speak," Sean said, and that caught everyone's attention.

"Sean, I don't think you've spoken at one of these meetings in three years," Sylvia said. "What's on your mind?"

"Rue, show them your stomach," Sean said.

She rose up on her knees and turned to look at him. "Why?" She was stunned and outraged.

"Just do it. Please. Show the Black Moon people."

"You'd better have a good reason for this," she said in a furious undertone.

He nodded at her, his blue eyes intent on her face.

With a visible effort, Rue faced the group and pulled down the front of her elastic-waist shorts. The Black Moon people looked, and Abilene gave a sharp nod of acknowledgment. Phil's dark eyes went from the ugly scar to Rue's face, and there was a sad kinship in them that she could hardly bear. Mustafa scowled, while Rick, David and Hallie looked absolutely matter-of-fact. Haskell, the enforcer, averted his eyes.

"The man who did this is out of the mental hospital, and he's probably here in the city," Sean said, his Irish accent heavier than usual. Rue covered her scars, sank to her knees on the floor and looked down at the linoleum with utter concentration. She didn't know if she wanted to swear and throw something at Sean or… she just didn't know. He had massively minded her business. He'd gone behind her back.

But it felt good to have someone on her side.

"I got a human to find a picture of this man in the newspa-per and copy it." Sean began to pass around the picture. "This is Carver Hutton IV. He's looking for Rue under her real name, Layla LeMay. He knows she dances. His family's got a lot of money. He can get into almost any party anywhere. Even with his past, most hostesses would be glad to have him."

"What are you doing?" Rue gasped, almost unable to get enough breath together to speak. "I've kept all this secret for years! And in the space of five minutes, you've told people everything about me. Everything!" For the first time in her life, Rue found herself on the verge of hitting someone. Her hands fisted.

"And keeping it secret worked out well for you?" Sean asked coolly.

"I've seen him," a husky voice said. Hallie.

And just like that, Rue's anger died, consumed by an over-whelming fear.

If any of the dancers had doubted Rue's story, they saw the truth of it when they saw her face. They all knew what fear looked like.

"Where?" Sean asked.

Hallie crooked her finger at her partner. "We saw him," she said to David. He put his white arm around her shoulders, and his dark, wavy hair swept over her neck as he bent forward.

"Where?" David asked Hallie.

"Two weeks ago. The bachelor party at that big house in Wolf Chase."

"Oh." David studied the picture a little longer. "Yes. He was the one who kept grabbing at you when you were on top. He said you were a bitch who needed to learn a lesson."

Hallie nodded.

Tiny shivers shook Rue's body. She made an awful noise.

"Jeez," Hallie said. "That's what he said to you, huh, when he cut you? We just thought he wanted us to do a little, you know, play spanking. We did, and he chilled. The host looked like he was upset with the guy's outburst, so we toned it down. Please the man who's paying the bill, right?"

David nodded. "I kept an eye on him the rest of the evening."

Sylvia said, "You watch out for this guy. That's all. Just let Rue know if you've seen him. Nothing else."

"You're the boss," Mustafa said. His voice was low and rumbly, like a truck passing in the distance. "But he will not hurt Abilene."

"Thanks, Moose," said the vampire. She stroked his dark cheek with her white hand. "I love ya, babe."

"Getting back on track," Sylvia said briskly. "Rick, you and Phil didn't turn in your costumes for a week after that Greek party. Hallie, you can't have your mail sent here. If you keep that up, I'll start opening it. Julie, you left the lights on in the practice room last night. I've talked to you about that before."

Sylvia read down a list of minor offenses, scolding and correcting, and Rue had a chance to calm herself while the other employees responded. She was all too aware of Sean standing behind her. She could not have put a label on what she was feeling. She went to sit on the high pile of mats that they sometimes spread on the linoleum floor when they were practicing a new lift.

When the others began leaving, Rue started to pull her outer layer of clothes back on.

"Not so fast," Sean said. "We have practice tonight."

"I'm mad at you," she said.

"Turn out the lights behind you, whichever one of you wins," Sylvia called.

Sean went out into the hall and locked the front door, or at least that was the direction his footfalls took. She heard him come back, heard him over at the big CD player in the corner, by the table of white towels Sylvia kept there for sweaty dancers.

Rue began to warm up, but she still wasn't about to look at Sean. She was aware he began stretching, too, on the other side of the room.

After fifteen minutes or so, she stood, to signal she was ready to practice. But she kept her eyes forward. Rue wasn't sure if she was being childish, or if she was just trying to avoid attacking Sean. He started the CD player, and Rue was startled to recognize Tina Turner's sultry voice. "Proud Mary" was not a thinking song, though, but a dancing song, and when Sean's hands reached out for hers, she had no idea what he was going to do. The next twenty minutes were a challenge that left her no time for brooding. Avril Lavigne, the Dixie Chicks, Macy Gray and the Supremes kept her busy.

And she never once looked up at him.

The next song was her favorite. It was a warhorse, and the secret reason she'd decided to become a dancer, she'd told him in a moment of confidence: the Righteous Brothers' "Time of My Life." She'd worn out a tape of the movie *Dirty Dancing*, and that song had been the climax of the movie. The heroine had finally gained enough confidence in herself and trust in her partner to attempt a leap, at the apex of which he caught her and lifted her above his head as if she were flying.

"Shame on you," she said in a shaky voice.

"We're going to do this," he said.

"How could you take over my life like this?"

"I'm yours," he said.

It was so simple, so direct. She met his eyes. He nodded, once. His declaration hit her like a fist to the heart. She was so stunned by his statement that she complied when he put his hand on her back, when he took her left hand and pressed it to his silent heart. Her right hand was spread on his back, as his was on hers. Their hips began to move. The syncopation broke apart in a minute as he began to sweep her along with him, and they danced. Nothing mattered to Rue but matching her steps to her partner's. She wanted to dance with him forever. At every turn of her body, every movement of her head, she saw something new in his pale face—a glint of blue eye, the arch of his brow, the haughty line of his nose, which contrasted so startlingly with the grace of his body. When the song began to reach its climax, Sean raced to one end of the long room and held out his hands to her. Rue took a deep breath and began to run toward him, thinking all the way, and when she was just the right distance from Sean, she launched herself. She felt his hands on her hipbones, and then she was high in the air above his head, her arms outstretched, her legs extended in a beautiful line, flying.

As Sean let her down the line of his body very slowly, Rue couldn't stop smiling. Then the music stopped, but Sean didn't let her feet touch the floor. She was looking right into his eyes, and the smile faded from her face.

His arms were around her, and his mouth was right by hers. Then it was on hers, and once again he asked admission.

Rue whispered, "We shouldn't. You're going to get hurt. He'll find me. He'll try to kill me again. You'll try to stop him, and you'll get hurt. You know that."

"I know this," Sean said, and he kissed her again, with more force. She parted her lips for him, and he was in her mouth, his arms surrounding her, and she was altogether overwhelmed. It appeared that she was his, as much as he was hers.

For the second time in her life, Rue gave herself up to some-one else.

"This is different," she whispered. "This is different."

"It ought to be." Sean said. "It will be." He picked her up in one smooth move. Their eyes were locked.

"Why are you getting into my life?" She shook her head, dazed. "There's so much bad in it."

"You fought back," he said. "You made a new life, on your own."

"Not much of one."

"A life with courage and purpose. Now, let me love you this way." His body moved against hers.

"I'm not scared." She was.

"I know it." He smiled at her, and her heart wrenched in her chest.

"You won't hurt me," she said with absolute faith.

"I would rather die." He was so serious.

"You know I can't have children," she said. She meant only to let him know he didn't need to use birth control.

"I can't, either," he murmured. "We can't reproduce."

If she'd ever known that, she'd forgotten it. She felt oddly jolted. She'd always supposed that her barrenness would be a terrible obstacle to forming another relationship, but instead it was a non-issue.

His tongue flicked in her ear. "Tell me what you like," he suggested, his breath tickling her cheek. He walked over to the pile of exercise mats, carrying her as if her weight was nothing.

"I don't know," she said, partly embarrassed at her own ignorance, partly excited because she was sure he would find out what she liked.

"Light out, light on?"

"Out, please."

In the space of a second, he was back beside her. He had a few towels with him. He spread them on the mats, and she was glad, because the vinyl surface was unpleasant to the touch.

"My clothes?" he asked. He waited for her answer.

"Oh...off." Ambient light came through the frosted glass in the door of the studio, and she could see the gleam of his skin in the darkness. He was built smooth and sleek, as dancers usually are, and he was purely white except for the trail of red hair starting below his navel and going down. She followed that trail with her eyes and found herself gasping.

"Oh...oh. Wow."

"I want you very much."

"Yeah, I get that." Her voice was tiny.

"Can I see you?" For the first time, his voice was tentative.

She sat up on the pile of mats and rose to her knees. She pulled off her white T-shirt very slowly, and her bra was gone in an instant.

"Oh," he said. He reached out to touch her, hesitated.

"Yes," Rue said.

His white hands with their long fingers cupped her breasts with infinite gentleness. Then his mouth followed.

She gasped, and it was an urgent sound. His hands began tugging her shorts, gathering up her panties with them, and she lay down so he could coax them over her feet. He stayed down there for a minute or two, sucking her toes, which made her shiver all over, and then he began working his way up her legs.

She was afraid her courage would run out. She wanted him so badly she shook all over, but her only previous experience with sex had been short and brutal, its consequences painful and disastrous.

Sean seemed to understand her misgivings, and he eased his body up her length until his arms wrapped around her and his mouth found hers again.

"I can stop now," he told her. "After this, I'm not sure. I don't want to hurt you or frighten you."

Rue said, "Now or never."

He gave a choked laugh.

"That didn't sound very romantic," she apologized. His hips flexed involuntarily, pressing his hard length against her stomach, and he began to lick her neck.

"Oh," she said, reaching down to touch him. "Oh, please." His fingers touched her intimately, making sure she was ready. The delicate movement of his fingers made Rue shudder.

Then he was at her entrance, the blunt head pushing, and then he was inside her. "Layla," he said raggedly.

"It's good," she said anxiously. After a few seconds, she said again, in an entirely different tone, "It's so good."

"I want it to be better than good." His hips began to move.

Then she couldn't speak.

# CHAPTER EIGHT

S HE HAD NEVER imagined she could be so relaxed, so content.

His hair had come loose from its ribbon and trailed across her breasts as he lay on his stomach looking down at her. He had never seen anything so beautiful as her face in the faint glow of the city night that lit the room through the frosted glass.

She wondered how he could have become so important to her in such a short time. She loved every line of his face, the power of his sleek white body, the passion of his lovemaking; but most of all she loved the fact that he was on her side. It had been years since anyone had been on her side, unconditionally, unilaterally. She thought, *I should still be angry that he went to Pineville.* But she searched for the anger she'd initially felt and found it was gone.

"I'm a wimp," she concluded, out loud.

"I know what that means," Sean said, his voice dreamy. "Why do you say that?"

"I'm glad you found out. I'm glad I don't have to tell you all about it. I'm glad you care enough to want to find...Carver."

The hesitation before she was able to say his name told Sean a lot.

"What did your parents do?" he asked. He hadn't had time to ask Will Kryder all the questions that had occurred to him.

"They didn't believe me," she murmured. "Oh, my brother Les stood by me. He saved me that night. But he's not a strong-willed, forceful kind of guy. See, my dad works for Carver's dad, and my dad probably couldn't get hired anywhere else now. He drinks a lot. I'm not sure he'd still have the job he's got if he wasn't my father. Dad knows Hutton's got to keep him on, or else he might talk. My mother...well, she decided to think it was a clever ploy on my part to get Carver to marry me. When she found out otherwise, she was...livid."

"She wanted you to marry him."

"Yes, she actually believed that I'd want to be tied to the man who raped me."

"In my time, we would have made him wed you," Sean said.

"Really?"

"If you were my sister, I would have made sure of it."

"Because no one else would have married me otherwise, right? Damaged goods."

Sean perceived he had made a massive error.

"And for the rest of my life I would have had to put up with Carver's little ways, like beating on me, because he'd raped me," Rue said coldly.

"All right, in my time, we would have been wrong," he conceded. "But we would have been on your side."

"I have you on my side," she said. "I have you on my side *now*. If this has meant anything to you."

"I don't get this close to anyone unless it means something to me."

"That come from being an aristocrat? In your time, were you like Carver?" There was an edge to her voice that hadn't been there before.

"The night we first make love, you can compare me to the man who raped you?"

She hadn't thought before she spoke. "After years of weighing every word I said to another person, all of a sudden I've gotten to be the worst—I'm so sorry, Sean. Please forgive me for the offense."

There was a long silence in the dark room. He didn't speak. Her heart sank. She'd ruined it. Her bitterness and mistrust had twisted her more than she knew. But she'd come by it naturally, and she didn't see how she could have existed otherwise.

After another unnerving two minutes of silence, Rue began to fumble around for her clothes. She was determined not to cry.

"Where are you going?" Sean asked.

"I'm going home. I've screwed up everything. You won't talk to me, and I'm going home."

"You offended me," he said, and his voice wasn't level or calm at all. He was saying, *You hurt me.* But Rue wasn't absorbing that. Before Sean could scramble into his own clothes, she was gone, wearing her flannel shirt tossed over her dance outfit. She'd thrust her feet into her boots without lacing them. She was out the door of the studio, then out the door to the building, before

Sean could catch her. He cursed out loud. He had to check the studio and lock everything up; that was the duty of the last person out, and it was something he couldn't shirk. He could always catch up with Rue, he was sure; after all, he was a vampire, and she was human.

———◆———

CARVER WAS waiting for her in the third alley to the north.

Rue was walking very swiftly. She was trying not to cry; and not having much luck. She wanted to reach the next corner in time for the bus, which would be the last one running on a Sunday night. As she passed the alley entrance, Carver burst out with such astonishing suddenness that he was holding her arm before she could react.

"Hello, Layla," he said, smiling.

The nightmares she'd had for four years had come to life.

Carver had always been handsome, but his present look was far from his preppy norm. He'd spiked his dark hair and he was wearing ragged jeans and a leather jacket. He'd disguised himself.

"I have a score to settle with you," he said, still smiling.

Rue hadn't been able to make a sound when he'd grabbed her arm, but now she began to scream.

"Shut up!" he yelled, and backhanded her across the mouth.

But Rue had no intention of shutting up. "Help!" she screamed. "Help!" She groped in her bag for her pepper spray with her free left hand, but this one night she hadn't been prepared, mentally or physically, and she couldn't find the cylinder she usually carried ready to use.

Pinning her with his grip on her right arm, Carver began pummeling Rue with his fist to make her shut up. She tried to dodge the blows, tried to find the spray, tried to pray that help would come. Where was the pepper spray? Abandoning her futile one-handed rummaging through her big bag, Rue yanked it off her shoulder, since it was only an impediment. Then she fought back. She wasn't nearly as big as Carver, so she went for his genitals. She wanted to grip and squeeze the whole package, but he pulled back. All she managed was a vicious pinch, but that was enough to double him over. When he heard a woman shouting from across the street, he staggered away from Rue.

"Leave that girl alone!" a female voice yelled. "I'm calling the police!"

Rue sank to her knees, too battered to stand any longer, but she stayed facing him, her hands ready to defend herself. She would not give up what she'd worked so hard to maintain. Carver began to hurry down the alley as swiftly as his injury would permit—she was proud to see he was walking funny—and though Rue remained upright, but still on her knees, he vanished from her sight as he passed out of the alley and onto the next street.

"I won't fall," she said.

"Are you okay?"

Rue wouldn't even take her eyes from the alley entrance to examine the woman beside her. This woman had saved her life, but Rue wasn't going to be taken by surprise again, if Carver decided to return.

"Rue! Rue!" To her immense relief, she heard Sean's voice. Now Carver couldn't hurt her anymore; no matter how angry

Sean was at her, he wouldn't let Carver strike her. She knew that. With profound relief, she understood she didn't need to stay vigilant any longer, and she sat back on the pavement. Then she was lying on the sidewalk. And then she didn't know anything else.

———◆———

WHEN SHE began to relate to her surroundings again, Rue knew she was in a strange place. Hospital? Nope, didn't smell like a hospital, a smell with which she was all too familiar. It was a quiet place, a comfortable place. She was lying on clean white sheets, and there was someone next to her. She tried to move, to sit up, and she found out she was sore in several places. Before she could gain control of herself, she groaned.

"You okay? You need a drink of water?" The voice was familiar and came from a few feet away. Rue pried her swollen eyes open. She could see—a little. "Is that Megan?" she asked, her voice a dry thread.

"Yep, it's me. Julie and I been taking turns."

"Who else is here? Where *is* here?"

"Oh, we're at Sean's place, in his safe room. That's him in the bed with you, babe. It's daytime, so he had to sack out. He wasn't going to leave you without someone to help you, though. He made us swear on a stack of Bibles that we wouldn't leave. So you won't think we're these wonderful people, I gotta tell you that he promised to help us out with the money we're getting docked for missing work. I mean, I want to help you, and I would've come, anyway. But I just couldn't, ah, skip telling you. Okay?"

Rue nodded. It was an effort, but somehow Megan caught the motion. "Water would be good," Rue managed to say.

In just a moment, Megan was sliding her arm under Rue's back and helping her sit up a little. There was a glass of cool water at her lips, and Rue sipped gratefully.

"You need to get up and go to the bathroom?"

"Yes, please."

Megan helped Rue rise. To her relief, Rue discovered she was in the T-shirt and shorts she'd worn the night before. She shuffled to the bathroom. When she was through, she washed her face in the sink and brushed her teeth with a toothbrush she found still encased in a cellophane wrapper. That made her feel a great deal better, and she made her way back to the bed with a little more confidence.

"Megan, I'll be okay now, if you need to get to work."

"You sure, girlfriend? I can stay. I don't want Sean to be mad at me."

"I'm good. Really."

"Okay then. It's four o'clock. Sean ought to be up in about two hours. Maybe you can get some more sleep."

"I'll try. Thank you so much."

"Don't mention it. See you later."

Rue had left the light in the bathroom on, and when Megan had gone through the heavy curtain at one end of the room, Rue turned to her silent companion. Sean lay on his back with his hair spread out on the pillow. His lips were slightly parted, his eyes closed, his chest still. The absence of that rising and falling, the tiny motion of life, was very unnerving. Did he know she was there? Did he dream? Was he truly asleep, or was he just held motionless, like a paralysis victim? She'd almost forgotten what they'd fought about. She stroked his hair, kissed his cool lips. She remembered what they'd done together, and a flush suffused her face.

What Carver had done to her, when he'd attacked her years before, didn't qualify as sex. It had been an assault, using his sex organ as the weapon. What she'd done with Sean had been real sex, making-love sex. It had been intimate and primal and wonderful. Carver had made her into a shell of a human being overnight. Over the course of a few weeks, Sean had helped her become a full person once more.

She wasn't going to chicken out just because he was dead part of the time.

So, when darkness fell, Rue made sure her arm was across his chest, her leg lying over his. Suddenly she knew he was awake. The next second, his body reacted.

"Good evening to you, too," she said, startled and intrigued by his instant readiness.

"Where is Megan?" he asked, his voice still a little fuzzy from sleep.

"I told her to go. I'm better."

His eyes widened as he remembered. "Show me," he demanded.

"You seem to be ready for anything," she said, greatly daring, her hand wandering down his abdomen in a tentative way.

"I have to see your injuries first," he said. "I shouldn't even be…it's your smell."

"Oh?" she tried to sound insulted, failed.

"Just the smell of you. Your skin, your hair. You make me hard."

Not a compliment she'd ever gotten before, but she could see the evidence of the sincerity of it.

"Okay, check me out," she said mildly, and lay down. Sean raised himself on one elbow, and his left hand began to turn her face this way and that.

"It's my fault," he said, his voice steady but not exactly calm. "I shouldn't have stopped to lock up the studio."

"The only fault is Carver's," she said. "I've played that blame game too many years. We don't need to start it all over again. For the first year after he attacked me, I thought, 'What if I hadn't worn that green dress? What if I hadn't let him hold my hand? Kiss me? Slow dance with me? Was it my fault for looking pretty? Was it my fault for treating him as I would any date I liked?' No. It was his fault, for taking a typical teenage evening and turning it into the date from hell."

Sean's fingers gripped her chin gently and turned her face to the other side so he could examine her bruises. He kissed the one on her cheek, and then he pulled the cover down to look over her body. She had to stop herself from pulling it right back up. This level of intimacy was great and very exciting, but she sure wasn't used to it.

"This is the closest anyone's been to me in years," she said. "I haven't even seen a doctor who looked at this much of me." Then she told herself to shut up. She was babbling.

"No one should ever see this much of you," he said absently. "No one but me." His fingers, whiter even than her own magnolia skin, brushed a dark bruise on her ribs. "How much are you hurting?"

"I'm pretty stiff and sore," she admitted. "I guess my muscles were all tensed up, and then, when I got knocked around…"

He touched her side gently, his hand very close to her breast. "Will you be able to dance tonight? We need to call Sylvia and cancel if you will not be able. She can get Thompson and Julie to do it."

He was still hard, ready for her. She was having a difficult time remembering her sore muscles.

"I don't know," she said, trying not to sound as breathless as she felt.

"Turn over," he said, and she obediently rotated. "How's your back?"

She moved her shoulders experimentally. "Feels okay," she said. His fingers traced her spine, and she gasped. His hand rubbed her hip.

"Don't think I got bruised there," she said, smiling into the pillow.

"What about here?" His hand traveled.

"There, either."

"Here?"

"Oh, no! Definitely not there!"

He entered her from behind, holding himself up so his weight wouldn't press on her tender ribs. "There?" he asked, the mischief in his voice making something in her heart go all soft and mushy.

"You'd better…massage…that," she said, ending on a gasp.

"Like this?"

"Oh, yes."

After they'd basked in the afterglow for a happy thirty minutes, Rue said, "I hate to bring this up, but I'm hungry."

Sean, stung by his own negligence, leaped from the bed in one graceful movement. Before Rue knew what was happening, he'd lifted her from the bed, ensconced her in a chair, and clean sheets were on the bed and the old ones stuffed in a hamper. He'd started the shower for her and asked her what kind of food she liked to eat. "Whatever's in the neighborhood," she said. "That's what I love about the city. There's always food in walking distance."

"When you come out of the shower, I'll be back with food for you," he promised.

"You haven't bought food in years, have you?" she said, and the fact of his age struck her in a way it hadn't before.

He shook his head.

"Will it bother you?"

"You need it, I'll provide it," he said.

She stared at him, her lips pressed together thoughtfully. He didn't say this like a wimp who was desperate for a woman. He didn't say it like a control freak who wanted to dole out the very air his sweetheart breathed. And he didn't say it like an aristocrat who was used to having others do his bidding.

"Okay, then," she said slowly, still thinking him over. "I'll just shower."

The heat of the water and the minutes of privacy were wonderful. She hadn't been around people on a one-on-one basis so much for some time, and to be precipitated into such an intimate relationship was quite a shock. An enjoyable one, but still a shock.

Having clean hair and a clean body did wonders for her spirits, and in the light of Sean's determination to provide for her, she found a pair of his jeans she could wriggle into. She rolled up the cuffs and found a faded pumpkin-colored T-shirt to wear. It was pretty obvious she wasn't wearing a bra, but she didn't know where her bra was. Rue had a terrible conviction that it was still in the studio, which would be a dead giveaway to the other dancers. She left the bedroom and went out into the living room/kitchen/office to wait for Sean. It was small and neat, too, and had a couple of narrow windows through which she could see people's feet go by. For the first time, she realized Sean had a basement apartment.

Shortly after, he came in with two bags full of food. "How much of this can you eat?" he asked. "I find I have forgotten." He'd gotten Chinese, which she loved, and he'd bought enough for four. Luckily, there were forks and napkins in the bags, too, since Sean didn't have such things.

"Sean," she said, because she enjoyed saying his name. "Sit down while I eat, please, and tell me about your life." She knew how his face looked when he came, but she didn't know anything about his childhood. In her mind, this was way off balance.

"While I was in Pineville," he said, "I looked in the windows of your parents' home. I was curious, that's all. In the living room, your father was staring into a huge glass case that takes up a whole wall."

"All my stuff," she said softly.

"The crowns, the trophies, the ribbons."

"Oh, my gosh, they still have all that out? That's just…sad. Did he have a drink in his hand?"

Sean nodded.

"Why did you tell me this when I asked to know more about you?"

"You're American royalty," he said, supplying the link.

She laughed out loud, but not as if he were really amusing.

"You are," he said steadily. "And I know you've heard Sylvia say I was an aristocrat. Well, that's her joke. My origins are far more humble."

"I noticed you could make a bed like a whiz," she said.

"I can do anything in the way of taking care of a human being," he said. He looked calm, but she could tell he wasn't— something about the way his hands were positioned on the edge of the table. "I was a valet for most of my human life."

## CHAPTER NINE

"**Y**OU WERE A gentleman's gentleman?" Her face lit up with interest.

He seemed taken aback by her reaction. "Yes, my family was poor. My father died when I was eleven, so I couldn't take over his smithy. My mother was at her wits' end. There were five of us, and she had to sell the business, move to a smaller cottage, and my oldest sister—she was fifteen—had to marry. I had to find work."

"You poor thing," she said. "To have to leave school so early."

He smiled briefly. "There wasn't a school for the likes of us," he said. "I could read and write, because our priest taught me. My sisters couldn't, because no one imagined they'd need to." He frowned at her. "You should be eating now. I didn't get you food so you could let it grow cold."

She turned her face down to hide her smile and picked up her fork.

"I got a job with a gentleman who was passing through our village. His boy died of a fever while he was staying at the inn, and he hired me right away. I helped out his valet, Strothers. I went with them when they returned to England. The man's name was Sir Tobias Lovell, and he was a strange gentleman. Very strange, I thought."

"He turned out to be a vampire, I guess."

"Yes. Yes, he was. His habits seemed very peculiar, but then, you didn't question people above you in social station, especially since anyone could see he was a generous man who treated people well. He traveled a great deal, too, so no one could wonder about him for too long. Every now and then, he'd go to his country house for a while. That was wonderful, because travel was so difficult then, so uncomfortable."

"But how did you come to be his valet? What happened to Strothers?"

"Strothers had already grown old in his service, and by the time I was eighteen, Strothers had arthritis so badly that walking was painful. Out of mercy, Sir Tobias gave him a cottage to live in, and a pension. He promoted me. I took care of his clothes, his wigs, his wants and needs. I shaved him. I changed his linen, ordered his bath when he wanted, cleaned his shoes. That's why I know how to take care of you." He reached over the table to stroke her hair. "Once I was in closer contact with Sir Tobias, it became obvious to me there was something more than eccentricity about the man. But I loved him for his goodness, and I knew I must keep his secrets, as much for my own sake as for his. We went on, master and man, for many years...maybe twelve or fifteen. I lost track, you see, of how old I was."

That seemed the saddest thing she'd ever heard. Rue lowered her gaze to hide her tears.

"I realized later that he'd take a little from the women he bedded," Sean said. "He pleased them very much, but most of them were weak the day after. In our small country neighborhood, he had the name of being a great womanizer. He had to go from one to another, of course, so no one woman would bear the brunt of his need. He seemed much healthier when we went to the cities, where he could visit houses of ill repute as much as he liked, or he could hunt in the alleys."

"What happened?"

"The village people grew more and more suspicious. He didn't age at all, you see, and people grew old very quickly then. But he lost money and couldn't afford to travel all the time, so he had to stay at the manor more often. He never went to Sunday church. He couldn't be up in the daytime, of course. And he didn't wear a cross. The priest began to be leery of him, though he donated heavily to the church.

"People began to avoid me, too, because I was Sir Tobias's man. It was a dark time." Sean sighed. "Then they came one night to get him, a few of the local gentry and the priest. I told him who was at the door, and he said, 'Sean, I'm sorry, I must eat before I run.' And then he was on me."

Rue had lost the taste for her food. She wiped her mouth and laid her hand over Sean's.

"He gave me a few swallows of his blood after he'd drained me," Sean said quietly. "He said, 'Live, if you have the guts for it, boy,' and then he was gone. The people at the front door broke in to begin searching the house for him, and they found me. They were sure I was dead. I was white; I'd been bitten, and they couldn't hear my heart. I couldn't speak, of course. So they buried me."

"Oh, Sean," she said, horror and pity in her voice.

"Lucky for me, they buried me right away," he said briskly. "In a rotten coffin, at that. Kept me out of the sunlight, and the lid was easy to break through when I woke." He shrugged. "They wanted to be through with the job, so they hadn't put me in too deep. And they didn't keep watch at the churchyard, to see if I'd rise. Another stroke of luck. People didn't know as much about vampires then as they did a hundred years later."

"What did you do after that?"

"I went to see my sweetheart, the girl I'd been seeing in the village. Daughter of the dry-goods dealer, she was." He smiled slightly. "She was wearing black for me. I saw her when she came out to get a bucket of water. And I realized I'd ruin the rest of her life if I showed myself to her. The shock might kill her, and if it didn't, I might. I was very hungry. Two or three days in the grave will do that. And I had no one to tell me what to do, how to do what I knew I must. Sir Tobias was long gone."

"How did you manage?"

"I tried to hold out too long the first time," he said. "The first man I took didn't survive. Nor did the second, or the third, or the fourth. It took me time to learn how much I could take, how long I could hold off the hunger before it would make me do something I'd regret."

Rue pushed her food away.

"Did you ever see him again?" she asked, because she couldn't think of anything else to say.

"Yes, I saw him in Paris ten years later."

"What was that like?"

"He was in a tavern, once again the best-dressed man in the place, the lord of all he saw," Sean said, his voice quite expressionless. "He always did enjoy that."

"Did you speak?"

"I sat down opposite him and looked him in the eye."

"What did he say?"

"Not a word. We looked at each other for a couple of minutes. There was really nothing to say, in the end. I got up and left. That night, I decided I would learn to dance. I'd done village dances as a boy, of course. I enjoyed it more than anything, and since I had centuries to fill and no pride to be challenged, I decided to learn all about dancing. Men danced then, almost all men. It was a necessary social grace if you were at all upper-class, and I could go from one group to another, acting like Sir Tobias when I wanted to learn the ballroom dances of the wealthy, and like my own class when I wanted to pick up some folk steps."

They both unwound as Sean talked about dancing. Rue even picked up her fork again and ate a few more bites. Gradually Sean relaxed in his chair and became silent. When she was sure he'd recovered from his story, she said, "I have to feed the cat. I need to go to my apartment."

"But you can't stay there," Sean said stiffly.

"Then where?"

"Here, of course. With me."

She did her best not to glance around the tiny apartment. She could probably fit her books and clothes in somewhere, but she would have to discard everything else she'd acquired with so much effort. How could they coordinate their very different lives? How much of his feeling for her was pity?

He could read her mood accurately. "Come on, let's get your things. If I'm right, you've missed one day of classes. You'll need to go tomorrow if you're able. How is walking?"

She was moving slowly and stiffly. Sean put socks on her feet and laced her boots in a matter-of-fact way. There was something so practical and yet so careful about the way he did such a lowly task that she felt moved in an unexpected way.

"At least I don't have a wig you have to powder," she said, and smiled.

"That was a great improvement of the twentieth century over the eighteenth," he said. "Hair care and shoes—they're much better now."

"Hair and shoes," she said, amusement in her voice. She thought that over while Sean got ready to go, and by the time they were outside in the night, she felt quite cheerful. She looked forward to lots of conversations with Sean, when he would tell her about clothes and speech patterns and social mores of the decades he'd lived through. She could write some interesting term papers, for sure.

She loved to listen to Sean talk. She loved it when he kissed her. She loved the way he made her feel like a—well, like a woman who was good in bed. And she loved the way he handled her when they were dancing, the respect in which he seemed to hold her. How had this happened over the past few months? When had he become so important to her?

Now, walking beside him, she was content. Though her life had just been shaken to pieces and her body was sore from a beating, she was calm and steady, because she had Sean. She loved every freckle on his face, his white strong body, his quirky mouth, and his dancing talent.

He'd done wonderful things for her. But he hadn't said he loved her. His blue eyes fixed on her face as if she were the most beautiful woman in the world, and that should be enough. The way he made love to her told her that he thought she was wonderful. That should be enough. She had a strong suspicion any man would laugh at her for wondering, but she wasn't a man, and she needed to hear the words—without having asked for them.

The next second she was yanked from her brooding by an unexpected sight. She'd glanced up at her apartment windows automatically, from half a block away, and she'd gotten a nasty shock.

"The light in my apartment is on," she said, stopping in her tracks. "The overhead light."

"You didn't leave it on last night?"

"No. The ceilings are high, and it's hard for me to change the bulbs in that fixture. I leave on the little lamp by my bed."

"I'll see," Sean said, pulling away from her grasp gently. She hadn't realized she'd been gripping his arm.

"Oh, please, don't go to the door," she said. "He might be waiting for you."

"I'm stronger than he is," Sean said, a little impatiently.

"Please, at least go up the fire escape, the one on the side of the building."

Sean shrugged. "If it'll make you happy."

She crept closer to the building and watched Sean approach the fire escape. He decided to show off at the last minute and scaled the brick wall, using the tiny spaces between bricks as hand- and toeholds. Rue was impressed, sure enough, but she was also disconcerted. It was unpleasantly like watching a giant insect climb. In a very short time, Sean had reached the level of the window and swung onto the fire escape. He peered inside. Rue could tell nothing from his stance, and she couldn't manage to see his face.

"Hey, Rue." Startled, she turned to see that her next-door neighbor, a part-time performance artist who called herself Kinshasa, had come up beside her. "What's that guy up to?"

"Looking into my apartment," she said simply.

"What were you doing last night? Sounded like you decided to rearrange the whole place."

"Kinshasa, I wasn't at home last night."

Kinshasa was tall and dreadlocked, and she wore big red-rimmed glasses. She wasn't someone you overlooked, and she wasn't someone who shrank from unpleasant truths. "Then someone else was in your place," she said. "And your friend's checking to see what happened?"

Rue nodded.

"I guess I should've called the cops last night when I heard all that noise," the tall woman said unhappily. "I thought I was doing you a favor by not calling the police or the super, but instead I was just being a typical big-city neighbor. I'm sorry."

"It's good for you that you didn't go knock on my door," Rue said.

"Oh. Like that, huh?"

The two stood watching as Sean came back down the fire escape in a very mundane way. He looked unhappy, so far as Rue could tell.

Sean, though not chatty or outgoing, was always polite, so Rue knew he had bad news when he ignored Kinshasa.

"You don't want to go back up there," he said. "Tell me what you need and I'll get it for you."

Suddenly Rue knew what had happened. "He got Martha," she said, the words coming out in a little spurt of horror. "He got her?"

"Yes."

"But I have to—" She started for the door of the building, thinking of all the things she needed, the fact that she had to find a box for the furry body, the grief washing over her in a wave.

"No," Sean said. "You will not go back in there."

"I have to bury her," Rue said, trying to pull away from his hand on her arm.

"No."

Rue stared up at him uncomprehendingly. "But, Sean, I have to."

Kinshasa said, "Baby, there's not enough left to bury, your friend is saying."

Rue could hardly accept that, but her mind skipped on to other worries. "My books? My notes?" she asked, trying to absorb the magnitude of the damage.

"Not usable."

"But it's four weeks into the semester! There's no way— I'll have to drop out!" The books alone had cost almost six hundred dollars. She'd gotten as many as she could secondhand, of course, but this late in the term, could she find more?

At least she had her dancing shoes. Some of them were in a corner at Blue Moon Entertainment, and the rest were in the bag she'd taken to Sean's. Rue's mind scurried from thought to thought like a mouse trapped in a cage.

"Clothes?" she mumbled, before her knees collapsed.

"Some of them may be salvageable," Sean murmured, but without great conviction. He crouched beside her.

"I know some people who can clean the apartment," Kinshasa said. "They just came over from Africa. They need the money."

This was an unexpected help. "But it's so awful in there, Sean says." Tears began to stream down Rue's face.

"Honey, compared to the mass graves and the slaughter they've had to clean up in their own country, this will be a piece of cake to them."

"You're right to give me some perspective," Rue said, her spine stiffening. Kinshasa looked as if she'd intended no such thing, but she bit her lip and kept silent. "I'm being ridiculous. I didn't get caught in that apartment, or I would've ended up like poor Martha." Rue managed to stand and look proud for all of ten seconds, before the thought of her beloved cat made her collapse.

"I'll kill him for you, honey," Sean said, holding her close.

"No, Sean," she said. "Let the law do it."

"You want to call the police?"

"Don't we have to? He'll have left fingerprints."

"What if he wore gloves the whole time?"

"I let him get away with hitting me last night, and what does he do? He comes here and kills my cat and ruins all my stuff. I should've called the police last night."

"You're right," Kinshasa said. "I'll call from my place right now." Sean said nothing, but he looked skeptical.

———◆———

THE POLICE were better, kinder, than Rue expected. She knew what that meant. Her apartment must be utterly gory. Sean told the detective, Wallingford, that he'd be able to tell what was missing. "You don't need to go up there," Wallingford told Rue, "if this guy can do it for you." Sean and Wallingford went up to the apartment, and Rue drank a cup of hot chocolate that Kinshasa brought her. Rue found herself thinking, *I've had friends around me all the time, if I'd just looked.*

When Sean reappeared with a garbage bag full of salvaged clothes, he told Rue the only thing he knew for sure was missing was her address book. "Was my address in it?" he asked her quietly.

"No," she said. "Maybe your phone number. But I didn't even know where you lived until last night."

"The police say you can go now. Let's go back to my place." After an uneasy pause, he continued. "Do you think you can dance tonight? It's almost too late to call Sylvia to get a replacement team."

"Dance tonight?" She looked at him as they walked, her face blank. "Oh! We're supposed to be at the museum tonight!"

"Ballroom dancing. Can you do that?"

"If there's a dress I can wear at the studio." Though she had to wrench her thoughts away from her destroyed apartment, it would be a relief to think about something else. They would waltz a little, do a dance number to "Puttin' on the Ritz." They'd done the same thing several times before. It was a routine that pleased an older crowd, which the museum benefactors were likely to be.

"They asked for us specifically," Sean said. But then he scowled, as if there were something about the idea he didn't like.

"Then we have to do it," Rue said. She was so numb, she couldn't have put into words what she was feeling. When Sean unlocked the studio, he insisted she stand outside while he checked it out first, and she did so without a word. He led her inside, looking at her eyes in a worried kind of way, trying to gauge her fitness. "Besides," Rue said, as if she was continuing a conversation, "I need the money. I have nothing." The enormity of the idea hit her. "I have *nothing*."

"You have me."

"Why?" she asked. "Why are you doing this?"

"Because I care for you."

"But," she said, disgusted, "I'm so weak. Look at me, falling apart—like I couldn't have predicted this would happen. Why did I even get a cat? I should have known."

"Should have known you shouldn't love something because it might be taken away from you?"

"No, should have known he'd kill anything I loved."

"Come on," Sean said, his voice hard. "You're going to put on the pretty dress here, and I'm going to make some phone calls."

The dress was the palest of pinks. It was strapless, with a full skirt. In the trash bag she found some matching panties to wear under it, and a paler pink frothy half slip. There were panty hose in the costume room, and Rue pulled on a pair. Her shoe bag was there, thank God, since she'd walked out in such a huff the night before, and it contained the neutral T-strap character shoes that would suit the program.

Sean, who'd finished his phone calls, pulled on some black dancer's pants and a white shirt with full sleeves. He buttoned a black vest over that and added his dancing shoes to Rue's bag. While he was buttoning the vest, he felt a brush running through his hair.

"Shall I braid it?" she asked, her voice so small it was barely audible.

"Please."

With the efficiency born of years of changing hairstyles quickly, Rue had his hair looking smooth and sleek in a minute.

"Will you leave yours loose?" Sean asked. "It looks beautiful as it is." Rue seldom left her long hair unbound for a performance, but he thought its color was brought out beautifully by the pale pink of the dress. "You look like a flower," he said, his voice low with admiration. "You would be wonderful no matter what you looked like, but your beauty is a bonus."

She tried to smile, but it faltered on her lips. She was too sad to appreciate his compliment. "It's nice to hear you say so," she said. "We need to go. We don't want to be late."

# CHAPTER TEN

T HEY TOOK A cab, which Sylvia would pay for; after all, they had to keep their clothes clean and fresh for the dancing. The Museum of Ancient Life had just opened a new wing, and the party was being held in the museum itself. All the attendees were patrons who'd donated very large sums toward the construction of the new wing. All of them were very well dressed, most of them were middle-aged or older, and they were all basking in the glow of being publicly acknowledged for having done a good thing.

The vampire and the dancer stood for a minute or two, watching limousines and town cars dropping off the well-heeled crowd. Then they made their way back to the entrance Sylvia had instructed them to use. The museum staffer at the door checked their names off a list. "Wait a minute," the heavy man said. "You're already here."

"Impossible," Sean said imperiously. "Here is my driver's license. Here is my partner's."

"Hmm," the man said nervously, his fingers drumming on the doorjamb. "I don't know how this happened. I shouldn't let you in."

"Then the Jaslows and the Richtenbergs will have to go without their dancing," Sean said. "Come, Rue."

Rue didn't have a clue what was happening, but she could tell Sean was quite indifferent that someone else had used his name, almost seemed to have been expecting it. If he was relaxed about it, so was she. "I'll call our employer on my cell," she said to the man. "You can explain to Sylvia Dayton that we're not being allowed entrance, so she won't blame us, okay?"

The man flushed even more, his eyes running up and down the printed list over and over, as if something different would pop up. When he glanced up at Sean and the vampire's eyes caught the guard's gaze, the man's face lost its belligerence instantly.

"I guess your names were checked off by mistake earlier. Come on in," he said.

Rue looked at Sean in awe. Vampire talents could come in handy.

It was lucky they'd dressed at the studio, because there wasn't a corner for them here. The back recesses of the museum weren't designed with parties in mind, as the Jaslows' home had been. The small rooms and narrow corridors were full of scurrying figures, and Rue realized that things were being handled by Extreme(ly Elegant) Events, Jeri's company, which had catered the Jaslows' party. The servers wore the traditional white jacket distinguished with the E(E)E logo on the shoulder. The halls were crowded with trays and trays of hors d'oeuvres, and cases and cases of champagne. Jeri was directing the staff, wearing the same serene smile.

And the man whose white jacket was straining across his shoulders was surely Mustafa, aka Moose, who worked for Black

Moon. As soon as she'd identified him, Rue realized that the short-haired woman opening a champagne bottle was Hallie, and her partner, David, was busy filling a tray of empty glasses. David looked quite different with his thick, wavy black hair pulled back and clubbed.

"Sean," she said, tugging on his hand to make him stop, "did you see Moose?"

He nodded, without looking around at her. They continued to make their way through the narrow maze of corridors to the door indicated on the little map Sylvia had left for them.

"Okay, this is it," he said, and they paused.

There was no place special to leave their bags, so they dropped them right inside the door, then changed into their dancing shoes on the spot.

"They're all here," he told her, when she was ready. "I called them. All of them who aren't working tonight, that is. Thompson and Julie have an early gig in Basing, and Rick and Phil have a very private engagement right after this for a few select museum patrons. But all the rest are here, even Haskell."

"Sylvia knows about this?"

"No. But that's so she can deny it."

"It's wonderful that they'd do this for you."

"They're doing it for you. Moose and Abilene gave our names to get in. The others came with the triple E people. When I heard the board had asked for us, specifically, I figured Hutton was behind it. We'll stop him tonight," Sean said, and then looked sorry he'd sounded so grim. "Don't worry, Rue." He kissed her on the check lightly, mindful of her lipstick.

Rue was too numb to grasp what Sean meant. Automatically, they checked each other over, Sean looked at his watch, and they swung open the door.

Since they were "on" the minute they stepped out of the door, they walked hand in hand with a light, almost prancing walk, until they'd reached the center of a huge open area. The dome stretched upward for three stories, Rue estimated. She'd been to the museum before—when the new wing had been under construction, in fact—and she loved the wide expanse of marble floor. Wouldn't their music get lost in the huge space?

Sean and Rue reached the center of the floor, Rue trying not to stare at the glass cases of masks that lined the wall. The dancers stood there, smiling, arms extended, waiting for all the milling patrons to become aware of their presence and to clear the area for their performance.

"Aren't they lovely!" exclaimed a white-haired woman with sapphire earrings who wasn't standing quite far enough away. A scowling face seemed to disagree. Rue dimly recognized the obnoxious man from the Jaslows' party, Charles Brody.

*Their music began over the public address system*, and Rue had to fight to keep her face pleasant. Sean had another surprise for her. He'd switched routines. The music was "Bolero." This was their sexy number, the one they'd only performed once or twice at anniversary parties. Why had he picked that music for this night?

But as they began to twine together in the opening moves, Rue seemed to be able to feel the sensuousness in her bones. She felt the passion, the yearning, conveyed by the music.

Suddenly Sean lifted her straight up, his hands gripping her thighs, until they formed a column. She looked down at him with longing, and he looked up at her with desire. She extended her arms gracefully upward as he turned in a smooth circle. As he continued to hold her, changing his grip so she was soaring above him like a bird, her full skirt falling over his shoulders, the crowd began to applaud at their display of strength and grace. Sean let her down so gradually that her feet didn't jolt when they touched the floor. She was able to pick up her steps again smoothly. Then Sean leaned her back, back, over his arm, and put his lips to her neck. She felt her whole body come alive when she felt his touch, and she waited for the bite with the faintest of smiles on her face.

But in that second, she was aware of a difference. Her partner was far tenser than he'd ever been at the finale; in fact, he was like an animal expecting attack. His body covered hers more completely than it should, as if he were protecting her. The crowd was closer than it should be, and she distinctly saw Haskell's face turn sharply to the right, his mouth opening to shout, allowing a glimpse of his shining fangs. A woman screamed.

Carver, in a tux, stepped out of the polite circle that had formed around the temporary dance floor, then he reached in his pocket and pulled out a knife. He pressed a button in the hilt and a wicked blade leaped out. In the space of a second, he'd slashed Haskell, who faltered and fell. Megan grabbed for Carver's arm next, and she might have slowed him down if Charles Brody hadn't shoved her as hard as he could, just as he'd done that night at the party. Again Megan landed on the floor, and then Carver was in the center of the circle with them.

She knew what he would do. She was sure that Sean thought Carver would try to kill her, and he might—if there wasn't anything else he could do to her—but first, she knew, he would try to kill Sean. Their just-finished dance had shown clearly that she loved the vampire, and Carver would relish killing something else she loved. Because Sean wasn't expecting it, she was able to shove him off her just as the knife descended.

Black-haired Abilene tackled Carver from the rear. Carver couldn't make a killing blow that way, but he managed to sink the knife into Rue's abdomen and pull it directly back out to strike again. Then a wounded Haskell, bloody and enraged, piled on top of Carver. With a bellow of enthusiasm, as if he were on the football field, Moose threw himself on top of them all.

The pain wasn't immediate. Unfortunately, Rue remembered all too clearly when he'd done the same thing years before, and she knew in a very short time she would hurt like hell. She made a bewildered sound as she felt the sudden wetness. Amid the screams and shouts of the crowd, Sean was trying to get Rue to her feet so he could drag her out of the melee. "He may have hired someone to help him. You have to get out of here," Sean said urgently.

But Rue watched Karl take a second to deck Charles Brody before he joined the other vampires in pinning Carver to the marble floor. The trapped man was fighting like a—well, like a madman, Rue thought, in a little detached portion of her brain. Not all the museum patrons had seen the knife, and they were bewildered and shouting. There could have been twenty assassins in the confusion of staff, patrons and servers.

"Come on, darling," Sean urged her, holding her as he helped her clear the outskirts of the gathering crowd. "Let's get out of here." He could feel her desperation and assumed he knew the cause. His eyes were busy checking the people moving around them, trying to be sure they were unarmed. "I thought if we did 'Bolero' we might provoke him to attack when we were ready for him, but this wasn't what I had planned." He laughed, a short bark with little humor.

Rue reached her free hand under her skirt and felt the wetness soaking her petticoats. It had begun trickling down her legs. She staggered after Sean for a few feet. She put her hand against a pillar to brace herself. When she lowered it to try to walk, she saw her perfect handprint, in blood, on the marble of the pillar. "Sean," she said, because he was still turned away from her, still looking for any other assault that might be coming their way.

He turned back impatiently, and his eye was caught at once by the handprint. He stared at it, his brow puckered as if he were trying to figure it out. He finally understood the tang of blood that he'd barely registered in his zeal to get Rue to safety.

"No," he said, and looked down at her skirt. If his face could become any whiter, it did.

His eyes looked like the lady's sapphire earrings, Rue thought, aware that she wasn't thinking like a rational person. But she figured that was probably a good thing. Because in just a minute the pain would start up.

"You're losing too much blood," he said.

"She's going to die," Karl said sadly. He'd materialized suddenly, pulling off his white jacket as he evaluated Rue's condition. "Even if you call an ambulance this minute, they will be too late."

"What…" For once, Sean seemed to be at a loss as to what to do.

"You have to hide her," Haskell said without hesitation, coming up to join them. The ordinarily tidy blond vampire, now disheveled and smeared with blood, was still cool-headed enough to be decisive. "If you want to save her, this is the last chance," he said.

"Find a place," Sean said. He sounded…afraid, Rue thought. She'd never heard Sean sound afraid.

Karl said, "The Egyptian room."

Sean picked Rue up like a child. Haskell and Karl followed, ready to ward off any attack from behind. But only a museum guard ran up to them, making some incoherent comment on Rue's wound. Haskell, clearly not in any mood for questions and maybe a little maddened by the scent of blood, pinched the man's neck until he slumped to the floor.

The Egyptian room had always been Rue's favorite. She loved the sarcophagi and the mummiform cases, even the mummies themselves. She'd often wondered about the ethics of exposing bodies—surely once people were buried, they deserved to stay that way—but she enjoyed looking on the long-dead features and imagining what the individual had been like in life—what she'd worn, eaten…who she'd loved.

Now Sean carried her to the huge sarcophagus in the middle of the floor. Made to contain the inner coffin of a pharaoh, the highly carved and decorated limestone sarcophagus was penned in by hard sheets of clear plastic, preventing people from touching the sides. Fortunately, this pen was open at the top. A vampire could clear the barrier easily.

Sean leaped over lightly, followed by Karl, while Haskell held Rue. Though the lid must have weighed hundreds of pounds, Karl and Sean easily shifted it to one side, leaving a narrow opening. Then Haskell carefully handed Rue to Karl, while Sean climbed in the deep stone box, which came to his lower chest. Karl handed Rue in, and Sean laid her on the bottom. She was able to lie flat on her back, with her legs fully extended. She felt as if she was looking up at Sean floating hundreds of feet above her. He lay down beside her, and she felt the numbness wearing away.

*Oh, God, no. Please.* She knew the onset of the pain. As she began to scream, Karl moved the lid back in place, and then there was almost perfect darkness.

———•———

"RUE," SAID Sean urgently.

She heard his voice, but the pain rendered it meaningless.

"Rue, do you want me to end the pain?"

She could only make a small sound, a kind of whine. Her fingers dug into him. There was hardly enough room side by side for them, and she had the feeling Sean couldn't straighten out, but that was the least of her concerns at the moment.

"You can be like me," he said, and she finally understood.

"Dying?" she said through clenched teeth.

"Yes. I wasn't quick enough. I didn't plan enough. And then you made sure he got you instead of me. Why, Rue? Why?"

Rue could not explain that she operated on instinct. She could not have borne to see the knife enter him, even though a moment's thought would have told her that he could survive what she could not. She hadn't had that moment. Her understanding was a tiny flicker in the bottom of a well that was full of agony.

"If I make you like me, you will live," he said.

This was hardly the best time to be making a huge decision, but she remembered the story Sean had told her about his master's sudden attack on him, the callous way the man had left Sean to cope with the sudden change. If Sean could survive such a metamorphosis, she could, because Sean was here to help her.

"Won't leave?" she asked. Her voice trembled and was almost inaudible, but he understood.

"Never." His voice was very firm. "If you love me as I love you, we'll weather the change."

"Okay." *Love*, she thought. *He loved her.*

"Now?"

"Now. Love you," she said, with great effort.

With no more hesitation, Sean bit her. She was already hurting so badly that it was just one more pain, and then she felt his mouth drawing on her, sucking her dry. She was frightened, but she didn't have the strength to struggle. Then, after a minute, the heavy grayness in her head rose up and took her with it.

"Here," said a voice, a commanding voice. "You have to drink, Rue. Layla. You have to drink, now." A hand was pressing her face to bare skin, and she felt something run over her lips. Water? She was very thirsty. She licked her lips, and found it wasn't water, wasn't cold. It was tepid, and salty. But she was very dry, so she put her mouth to the skin and began to swallow.

———◆———

SHE WOKE again sometime later.

She felt...funny. She felt weak, yes, but she wasn't sore. She remembered vividly waking up in the hospital after the last time she'd been attacked, feeling the IV lines, the smell of the sheets, the little sounds of the hospital wing. But it was much darker here.

She tried to move her hand and found that she could. She patted herself, and realized she was a terrible mess. And there was someone in this dark place with her. Someone else who wasn't breathing.

Someone *else*...who wasn't breathing.

She opened her mouth to scream.

"Don't, darling."

*Sean.*

"We're...I'm..."

"It was the only way to save your life."

"I remember now." She began shivering all over, and Sean's arms surrounded her. He kissed her on the forehead, then on the mouth. She could feel his touch as she'd never felt anyone's touch before. She could feel the texture of his skin, hear the minute sound of the cloth moving over his body. The smell of him was a sharp arousal. When his mouth fell on hers, she was ready.

"Turn on your side, angel," Sean said raggedly, and she maneuvered to face him. Together, they worked down her panty hose, and then he was in her, and she made a noise of sheer pleasure. Nothing had ever felt so good. He was rougher with her, and she knew it was because she was as he was, now, and his strength would not hurt her. Her climax was shattering in its intensity. When it was over, she felt curiously exhausted. She was, she discovered, very hungry.

She said, "When can we get out?"

"They'll come lift the lid soon," he said. "I could do it myself, but I'm afraid I'd push it off too hard and break it. We don't want anyone to know we were here."

In a few minutes, she heard the scrape of the heavy lid being moved to one side, and a dim light showed her Rick and Phil standing above them, holding the heavy stone lid at each end.

Other hands reached down, and Julie and Thompson helped them out of the sarcophagus.

"How is it?" Julie asked shyly, when she and Rue were alone in the women's bathroom. The men were cleaning up all traces of their occupancy of the sarcophagus, and Rue had decided she just had to wash her face and rinse out her mouth. She might as well have spared the effort, she decided, evaluating her image in the mirror—delighted she could see herself, despite the old myth. Her clothes were torn, bloody and crumpled. At least Julie had kindly loaned her a brush.

"Being this way?"

Julie nodded. "Is it really that different?"

"Oh, yes," Rue said. In fact, it was a little hard to concentrate, with Julie's heart beating so near her. This was going to take some coping; she needed a bottle of TrueBlood, and she needed it badly.

"The police want to talk to you," Julie said. "A detective named Wallingford."

"Lead me to him," Rue said. "But I'd better have a drink first."

It wasn't often a murder victim got to accuse her attacker in person. Rue's arrival at the police station in her bloodstained dress was a sensation. Despite his broken arm, Carver Hutton IV was paraded in the next room in a lineup, with stand-ins bandaged to match him, and she enjoyed picking him from the group.

Then Sean did the same.

Then Mustafa.

Then Abilene.

Three vampires and a human sex performer were not the kind of witnesses the police relished, but several museum patrons had seen the attack clearly, among them Rue's old dance partner, John Jaslow.

"There'll be a trial, of course," Detective Wallingford told her. He was a dour man in his forties, who looked as though he'd never laughed. "But with his past history with you, and his fingerprints on the knife, and all the eyewitness testimony, we shouldn't have too much trouble getting a conviction. We're not in his daddy's backyard this time."

"I had to die to get justice," she said. There was a moment of silence in the room.

Julie said. "We'll go over to my place so you two can shower, and then we can go dancing. It's a new life, Rue!"

She took Sean's hand. "Layla," she said gently. "My name is Layla."

# Layla
# Steps Up

T HE MUSIC WAS an eerie solo on a South American
pipe, sinuous and curling back on itself, the same way
that the two dancers entwined. Sean O'Rourke and Layla LeMay
never got farther apart than an arm's length, never lost contact.
His arm wound around hers, her leg wrapped around him while
her arms arced backward, and then she climbed up his body,
ending with her waist gripped by Sean, her legs straight up in
the air. After holding this torturous pose for a long moment,
Layla swung downward to land in front of Sean, her back to
him. He wrapped both his arms around her, her hands covered
his, and his lips grazed her neck. The music came to a stop on
a quavering note.

Although this was only a practice session for the Valentine's
Day exhibition, "Love, Sex, and the Dance," there were a few
patrons and dancers sitting in the auditorium. There was a smattering of applause.

Layla lay back against Sean with her eyes closed for a few
seconds and then she stepped away, switching her grip to hold

his hand and stand beside him while they took a bow and left the stage.

Layla was very pleased. The sinuous duet was by far the most demanding routine they'd ever done. It beat doing a two-step at a charity ball, for sure.

"My woman," Sean said, giving her a kiss.

"My man." She put her hand on his cold cheek.

The partners were the only vampire team working for Blue Moon Entertainment. The other dance teams were all vampire/human, as Sean and Layla had been a year ago.

Backstage, Sylvia Dayton, the human owner of Blue Moon, gave them a thumbs-up. Sean nodded, and Layla sketched a curtsy.

"That's *totally* appropriate for the exhibition," Sylvia said in a low voice, when Thompson and Julie's music came on. The two dancers now on stage presented a distinct contrast: Thompson's mother had been Polynesian, and he had remained a golden color after his first death. Julie was blonde, and warm-blooded.

The tango music made Layla sway, and she watched the couple dance for a minute or two. When Layla noticed Sean was ready to go, she smiled apologetically and they returned to the dressing room to put on their street clothes.

"Time to call a donor," Sean said as he zipped up his pants. "You must be hungry." Layla had met her first death only a year before, and she had to eat more frequently than Sean, who was working on his third century.

"Shall I get two?" Layla pulled her phone from her purse. The volunteer donors' bureau in Rhodes had a long list of humans who would give blood to vampires for a nominal sum. In return, the vamps would make the experience *very* pleasant. The contract each client vampire signed with the bureau stated the parameters of the transaction very clearly.

"I suppose so," Sean said. He was pulling on his boots.

Layla paused with her finger over the speed dial number. "What's the matter?" she asked. Sean was her maker, and though she knew him better than anyone else, she could not always be sure what he was thinking. But she knew he was not excited, or even pleasantly anticipatory.

"It still seems unnatural to order up blood instead of hunt for it," he said, his Irish accent making everything sing in Layla's ears. "And it makes life almost too easy."

What he left unspoken was his very different experience during his first year as a vampire. Layla had never experienced the necessity of sticking to the shadows, attacking the unwary, fearing exposure with every feeding, constantly looking for a safe place to sleep for the day.

Sean had only described it as frightening. It had never occurred to her that he believed she had missed something.

"Isn't this better for everyone?" Layla asked. Her hand gripped the phone so tightly that she realized she might crush it. She often forgot how strong she was now.

"I'm sure it is," Sean said, without conviction.

"You want to go hunting old-style? That would be stimulating for you?" She felt as if a dark pit had opened under her feet. For the past year, while she had adjusted to being dead, Layla had thought she and Sean had been perfectly happy.

"Darling, I would not endanger you," Sean said. "If I were caught taking from someone unwilling, if I killed someone, the consequences to you would be too harsh."

"They would? Why?" Layla heard an edge in her voice, and she knew her eyes had narrowed. For the past few weeks, she'd had the uneasy suspicion there was a lot she didn't know about her altered state. Yet she'd been content enough, and she hadn't worried about it. Until now.

"You would be left alone." Sean had his back to her as he buttoned his coat. Layla wished she could have read his face when he said that.

*You would be left alone.* Layla chewed that over as they left the auditorium. Obviously, she'd be alone if something happened to Sean. But she detected an implication to his words, a nuance beyond the obvious. Layla wondered what he was really telling her.

Sean had turned her to save her life. A stalker who'd been pursuing Layla had finally had a chance to strike at her. Luckily for Layla, he'd attacked her in a public place with plenty of witnesses, and they'd pulled him away in time to save her life…barely. Sean had determined that her blood loss was probably fatal, so he had turned her. They'd been a couple before her death; Layla looked forward to being a couple for hundreds of years.

But as the two walked silently together in the direction of their apartment, Layla mulled over her sense of unease. It appeared that her assumption that life—well, death—was perfect, wasn't shared by Sean. But she didn't know what to do about it.

Rubio, the doorman at the vampire-owned apartment building, greeted them by name. He was a vampire himself, of course.

During the day, armed humans stood guard. Sean and Layla paid for the extra security, and it gave them peace.

Thirty minutes after after Sean and Layla unlocked their apartment door, Rubio called to tell them the donors had arrived. Part of Rubio's job was to check the donors' credentials, and he'd never neglected to be sure they were legitimate. When the knock came at the door, Sean answered it. Layla, brushing her just-washed hair in front of the bedroom mirror, heard Sean say, "Good evening." She came into the living room as he was extending his hand to the female donor.

Usually, if a couple turned up, she would take the woman and Sean would take the man. Not tonight. Layla felt another frisson as Sean talked to the woman, but she was hungry enough to ignore it for the moment.

The male donor's eyes widened when he saw her. He clearly felt he'd hit the jackpot. Layla knew she was beautiful; people had been telling her so since she was a teenager. Layla's skin was not yet the bleached white of the older vampires, her hair was a rich mahogany that fell below her shoulder blades, and her eyes were almost the same color as her hair. Her features were absolutely symmetrical.

Groomed by her driven mother, Layla had competed in beauty pageants for all of her short human life, and she'd earned a college scholarship that she'd never gotten to use. But her beauty had also nearly been the death of her—in a way, it had been the death of her—and Layla never forgot that.

The donor introduced himself as Calvin. He had to be at least twenty-one to qualify for the program, but he looked younger. Calvin might have a good job, but his geeky looks endeared him to Layla, who had been a college student when she died.

*The least I can offer him is some enthusiasm.* Layla smiled brilliantly as she drew him closer. She tried to keep her eyes focused on his face so she could ignore the visible sign that he was very glad to meet her.

"You don't want to lie down?" Calvin said hopefully.

"Standing is good," she said. "You'll see."

Layla was tall enough to reach his neck easily, and she licked the spot first, feeling him jerk and gasp. Then she bit, softly, and willed him to be blissful with the pain.

His blood made her soar. Between feedings, she eked out her nutrition by drinking one of the artificial blood drinks, but it was like guzzling Thunderbird instead of champagne.

Over Calvin's shoulder, Layla kept an eye on Sean, still talking to his donor, who had introduced herself as Sue. Sue had clearly been impressed by Sean, who (though not conventionally handsome) appealed to a certain group of women. The Irish accent, the blade of a face, the long red hair…yes, he had some admirers. When he embraced Sue, she leaned into him. She jerked when he bit, jolted with pleasure. Her arms tightened around Sean, and her eyes shut.

When Sean and Layla finished feeding, almost simultaneously, they each kissed their donors on the cheek. "Keep safe," Layla said to Calvin, who didn't seem to be in any hurry to leave. Neither did Sue. Layla sighed inwardly and began herding the donors toward the door, smiling and talking the whole time. Calvin begged her to request him the next time she called the bureau, and Sue pressed her phone number into Sean's hand.

After Layla locked the door behind them, she turned to Sean, who had only been waiting to be alone with her. When he kissed her, she responded ardently. Coasting high on the infusion of fresh blood, they couldn't wait to get to the bedroom. The living room floor was good enough.

Layla had learned everything she knew about consensual sex from Sean. Tonight she tried something Abilene, a sex performer, had described. Following Abilene's advice, she crawled down Sean's torso to part his legs and licked the skin behind his balls before grazing that spot with her fangs.

Sean's reaction was nothing short of explosive. Afterward, he gave her a deep kiss and held her. He said, "That was the best sex I've had in a hundred years."

Layla laughed, proud she had made him so happy. She made a mental note to thank Abilene later. Abilene was an expert at her job, and she was the strongest woman (or vampire) that Layla knew. Layla would never have predicted they'd become friends when they'd first met. She'd shied away from the Black Moon people, and she felt ashamed of that now.

As she sat curled up with a book a bit later, Layla, relaxed and boneless, told herself that she'd imagined Sean's restlessness—he surely loved her.

She could not imagine living without him. It terrified her to think of such a thing. She'd been worrying away at Sean's earlier statement, and she'd figured out what had concerned Sean when he'd said, "You'd be left alone."

He didn't think she could survive.

Layla half-smiled. She recalled a pageant in Memphis, Miss Cotton Boll. She had just come off stage after her talent (dancing, of course), and she'd been dabbing her face with a towel when Carla Summers, Miss Dixie Belle, had launched herself at Layla with a pair of scissors, screaming, "You used my music!" Without hesitation, Layla had pulled up her knee and kicked Carla in the belly with all of her strength, simultaneously throwing her towel in Carla's face to blind her. One of the pageant moms had caught the whole thing on her phone. In return for Layla's promise not to prosecute, Carla had retired from the pageant circuit that night.

Layla felt fully capable of defending herself.

———◆———

THE AUDITORIUM was booked for another event the next night, so a general practice was scheduled at the Blue Moon/Black Moon studio. Layla and Sean were in their rehearsal clothes and warming up by the time Thompson and Julie straggled in.

Layla thought of Julie as a friend, but the blonde didn't seem to be feeling the same warmth. She nodded briefly at Layla's greeting and crossed the room to warm up at the opposite barre, as far away from Layla as she could get. *Everybody has an off night*, Layla told herself, refusing to be hurt for so small a reason.

Layla was excited about the practice, which was to be conducted by Feodor, the dance master Sylvia had hired for the Valentine Day exhibition. Sylvia was willing to invest in the future: she saw that the novelty of having vampire dancers at fund-raisers and private parties was subsiding. If this presentation was successful (and the event had already sold out), Sylvia would keep Feodor on staff.

The Russian had been trained classically at the Bolshoi decades ago, and it had stunned all of the Blue Moon dancers when they'd found out he was going to be Abilene's partner. No one had known that the sex performer was a fine ballerina. And none of them knew how Feodor had met Sylvia, who'd only lived a fraction of his life. The vampire was deceptively sleek, an icy blond with pale blue eyes. He carried a cane to practice. He'd slash out with it if he felt a dancer was not working hard enough.

Tonight, Feodor had apparently decided to take their minds off tomorrow night's opening performance. He led them in a series of combinations. The aged Russian vampire demonstrated steps that Layla had never seen. She doubted anyone had, in decades.

Layla focused intently. From the corner of her eye she saw that Abilene was following Feodor's instructions with apparent ease, her angular face expressionless. Some of the troupe members were unhappy that a sex performer was getting a plum position on the program, but Layla was sure that Abilene, no matter how she earned her money now, had at some point been an established ballerina.

"You're lazy, lazy, *lazy!*" Feodor snarled, whacking Thompson on the back of his thigh.

"Ouch," Layla whispered sympathetically as Thompson took a position at her right side.

He glared at her. "Better lazy than a leech like you," he muttered.

Layla's eyes opened wide, but before she could react to the accusation, Feodor rapped out a new set of instructions. She had to leap (literally) to comply.

Sean had overheard Thompson's insult. Vampires could hear the merest whisper. *As if the evening hasn't already been stressful enough*, Layla thought. Sean's blue eyes were narrow, his face set in rigid lines as he contained his anger during the class.

When they had a five-minute break, Layla asked, "What the hell was that about? Do you know?"

"I'll kill the bastard."

"I don't understand. Does he think I'm living off you?" She contributed most of her income to their common account, although she put a small sum aside every month to save enough to resume taking night classes. (Continuing her program at the university had not been possible after her death.)

"Don't worry, darling. You're right as rain."

But Layla didn't feel "right as rain." To regain control she recited her mother's mantra: *Head up, chest out, shoulders square, big smile, pretty hands.* Her mother had whispered those words in Layla's ears every time she'd taken the stage at a pageant.

And, smiling brightly, Layla got through the rest of the session.

The minute that practice was over, Layla pulled on her coat and boots, hoping that Sean would follow suit. But Sean was clearly determined to confront Thompson, and he waited for all the other dancers to leave.

Julie was waiting for her partner. Thompson glanced at Sean and said, "Julie, can you walk home by yourself tonight?"

"No, I'm staying," the blonde said. She glared at Layla as if she'd been the offender.

Sean stepped up Thompson, got right in his face. "Talk to Layla like that again and I'll punch you bloody," Sean said. There was no doubting his sincerity.

Thompson was no coward. "Your wife is not worthy of being a vampire," he said. "She's had a year to become strong. When the parting comes, she'll flounder and die. You shouldn't coddle her. You'll lose your opportunity."

"Parting?" Layla could hardly decide what question to ask first. "What opportunity?" She looked to Sean for an explanation, but he was glaring at Thompson.

"You and Sean will split up soon," Thompson told her. At least he didn't sound happy about it.

Layla would not have believed him if Sean hadn't stood there silently.

"No vampire couple stays together for long, if one has turned the other. That's the way it works." Thompson shrugged.

"Not always," Sean said, at Layla's side and with his arm around her. "And not us." No one said anything else for a long moment. Then Sean turned his back on Thompson. "Sweetheart, will you be braiding my hair?"

Layla, who felt as if she was wandering through a bad dream, picked up a brush and began to work on his long hair, bright and silky and flaming red. She made her back stiff and her face still. She would not break down, not in front of Thompson, not in front of Julie, who was looking at Layla as though she pitied her. That bit worst of all.

After the door slammed shut behind the two, Layla said in a very quiet voice, "Is that true? Will you leave me? You do think I'm too weak to make it on my own, though I don't know why. And what exactly am I keeping you from?"

She'd tied off his braid. She gripped his shoulders and forced him to turn to her.

Sean met her eyes. "At first, I didn't realize you didn't know the tradition. A maker and his child can't maintain a marital relationship for very long, and a year is the normal...honeymoon period." He looked down, breaking their connection. "I hoped the time would pass, and we would still be together. I couldn't bear to tell you such a terrible thing."

"You hoped my *ignorance* would leave me happy? That it would be okay if I didn't know something *every other vampire* around me knew? Something directly affecting *my life?*" She trembled with rage.

"Layla LaRue LeMay," he said sharply.

"Am I supposed to leap to attention because you used my whole name?" Something vast and cold stirred inside her. "Do you have any respect for me at all?" She felt the hairs on her arms stand on end as she went on full alert.

Sean was clearly shocked. "Can I talk to you for a moment without you snapping at me?"

"Speak," she snapped.

"I didn't want you worrying about something that might never happen. I thought you'd pick over every little thing, wondering if it meant the beginning of the end."

"That's exactly what I'm doing now. Tell me the truth."

"It's true that if a vampire turns a human and the two are lovers, often the relationship doesn't last more than a year, maybe two."

For the first time since she'd woken up dead, Layla wanted to pulverize something, anything.

"But we can be the exception," he said. "I love you more than I've loved anything or anyone in my life."

*How can I argue with that?* Layla thought. But she didn't melt against him. She put her hand on his shoulder to keep him away. "Sean, I managed to live through a lot when I was human. I'm proud of that. I got away from a terrible situation. I recovered from terrible injuries. I was educating myself, supporting myself. Whatever I am, it isn't *weak*."

"I know, darling," Sean said, suspiciously eager to close the subject. "Don't worry about what Thompson said. He's never had a lover who lasted longer than two months, right?"

Layla managed to relax, but it felt like stepping back from a high drop. Her fists were clenched so tightly that her palms were bleeding. She'd almost hit Sean. She would have enjoyed doing so. With some effort, she subdued the expanding chill of rage inside her.

The shadows in the corner of the room moved. Layla was surprised to see Feodor was there. The Russian was so ancient that he could be almost invisible, something she'd never seen or imagined. Feodor said, "Someone as beautiful as your wife deserves the truth. I believe she can defend herself."

"Thank you, Feodor," Layla said, startled at Feodor's presence. Why did the Russian care about her relationship problems? She was surprised he even had an opinion about her ability.

Sean was even angrier at a second intrusion. "My woman is my concern, Feodor. Layla was a delicate woman, and she is a fragile vampire. But she has great heart."

Feodor didn't respond, but faded away in a disconcerting fashion. The long walk home was thick with unspoken words. They were silent until they turned onto their street. Sean said, "You are just as beautiful as you were the night I met you."

No matter how frustrated Layla was, she had to smile at Sean. She thought his mouth was delightful. When he smiled, the corners came up in a way that made her heart ache, like a letter M. She knew she loved Sean, but she also suspected he didn't really respect her. She was turning that suspicion over in her head.

"You were pretty skeptical about me when we met," she said. "You didn't want to be my partner." She was watching her footing. The pavement was still dotted with patches of snow.

"Ah, I didn't know you, sweetheart." They walked for a moment in silence, passing a phalanx of cars parked at the curb. Parking was a premium in the older neighborhoods. Though all these vehicles were cold and silent, somewhere nearby Layla heard an idling car. Nothing moved on the streets. It was after 2 a.m.

"It's true I've never had to deal with the fear of being exposed," Layla said. All the vampires born before the past few years had feared being found in the daylight more than anything else.

"The effort to conceal your true nature is very...suspenseful. I had no advice or help at all when I came over. It was a terrible time." Sean's expression was bleak. Sean's maker had drained him for a jolt of energy, and literally fled the scene to avoid being staked by suspicious townspeople. He visibly banished his bad memories and looked at Layla with determination. "You don't need to be killing and ripping and having territory fights, Layla. Not with us being together."

For once, the Irish accent didn't make his words charming. Layla couldn't unhear the subtext. *"You won't be hurt. Not as long as I'm protecting you."* When had he decided she was "delicate"? That was what he'd told Feodor.

A long black limo passed them and coasted to a halt at the light at the next corner. Someone coming home from a fancy club, or maybe a show and dinner? They hardly lived in an upscale neighborhood. Somehow, on the lonesome night street, the darkened windows of the limo seemed sinister. When the light changed, it passed on slowly.

Though she noted the limo and thought it was out of place, Layla was preoccupied. She faced a new reality. She'd been walking through her life blindfolded, content with the status quo after the terrible years of living in fear of her stalker. She and Sean danced together, rehearsed together, had friends in common. They called donors. And they fed from each other during sex, which was incredible.

*At least to me.* Before she'd met Sean, the only sexual experience she'd had was a brutal rape. What she had with Sean was deeply satisfying. She knew Sean had had centuries to develop a sophisticated taste, and he'd certainly been excited by Abilene's little trick. But for the first time, Layla thought, *Am I boring?* The idea bit at her.

"We'll be grand." Sean had obviously been following his own train of thought. He sounded as if he were convincing himself. "And if Thompson says anything of that nature to you again, I'll take him apart." He nodded sharply as if to say, *There, that's settled.*

A black limo passed by them again. Layla thought it was odd they'd seen two similar cars so late at night, but she'd had another new thought as she reinterpreted Feodor's words. Feodor was hinting she should have taken Thompson apart herself.

That was how vampires proved their strength; they didn't wait for someone to defend them. Layla had not been identifying herself as a vampire; she'd been sleeping during the day, awake at night and drinking blood, but she hadn't truly come to terms with her new state of being. Inside, she'd still been Layla LaRue LeMay, pageant queen from Tennessee. She hadn't tapped into the power of her transformation.

No wonder they all thought she was weak.

She was still turning this new idea over when she climbed into bed. While Sean was absorbed in his latest book purchase, a thriller, Layla turned on her side away from him, and pondered. She could hear and smell and taste things that she hadn't when she was breathing. She knew that, at least theoretically, she was incredibly strong, incredibly powerful. But she'd never had to call on her strength and cunning in the hunt, she'd never had to call on her senses to hide, and she'd never had to disguise what she was. Layla wondered if those were the stressors that triggered the true vampire nature. She remembered the feeling that had flooded through her earlier, when Thompson had insulted her. She'd felt a hint of the power she hadn't tapped.

Her last thought before the sun rose was *I really am a wimp.*

The next night, Sean and Layla had to hurry to the auditorium for the dress rehearsal. All the patrons, students from the university dance classes, and a few other people had been invited to attend.

Layla wanted to talk to Sean as they walked, but she wasn't sure what to say. The revelation that she must seize her new role or forego any respect from her peers left her stymied. She didn't want to jump on some innocent human and drain him dry, just to prove herself qualified to be a vampire. But her lack of gumption was not only reflecting poorly on her, but also on Sean, apparently. Sean, who'd been on the phone while she dressed, seemed just as lost in his thoughts as she was. They entered the stage door in an uneasy silence. Layla felt relieved that she'd have to focus on the mechanics of the duet.

Just inside the door, Sean stopped dead. He even pulled on Layla's arm to get her to backpedal.

A woman she'd never seen before was talking to Sylvia just inside the door. Since Sylvia normally didn't let outsiders back-stage before a performance, the tall woman was likely to be a very generous patron.

Before they could leave (if that was what Sean intended), Sylvia noticed them and beckoned them forward. "Hi, you two!" Sylvia said cheerfully. "Got a minute?"

Under Layla's hand, Sean's arm was as hard as a stick of fire-wood, and she could feel the tension vibrating through him.

"Layla, this is Margo DeCordova, one of our platinum con-tributors," Sylvia told them. "She's just returned from a long stay in Europe. Sean, you remember Margo, of course?"

Sean stood silent. Layla had to take the lead. "Thanks so much for your generosity," she said to the woman, with her best pageant smile. "We're having so much fun with this event, and you've made it possible."

Margo DeCordova gave Layla the most minimal upturn of the lips. Her attention was fixed on Sean. "Oh, Sean and I know each other," Margo said.

"Mrs. DeCordova," he said, with a miniscule dip of the head.

"It's been a long time." From the way Margo said those words, Layla knew the woman had had sex with Sean.

This was horribly unpleasant, though inevitable, since Sean had led a long life before meeting Layla. But Layla had learned to conceal her emotions in a tough school. Her gleaming pageant smile remained fixed on her face. She glanced sideways at her partner, hoping he would break his silence, but Sean seemed frozen. This woman had him spooked.

At first glance, Layla couldn't see the danger. Margo was middle-aged, very groomed and toned. Her hair was an unobtrusive and well-bred blond, her suit was expensive without being extravagant, and her makeup and jewelry were understated. Margo gave the impression of being a civilized woman. But when Layla reached Margo's eyes, she understood. If Margo could have dug a spoon into Sean and eaten him, she would have.

Later, Layla could not recall any of the conversation after that. Sean remained stubbornly silent. Finally, Layla said, "Nice to talk to you two, but we have to get ready, and we're running late." After a long moment, Margo and Sylvia stepped aside so they could pass.

Sean led Layla past them with almost offensive haste. The confrontation—if it had been that—was over.

Layla felt a rush of relief as they reached the safety of the dressing room. Perhaps, while they changed into their practice clothes, Sean might explain his reaction to Margo DeCordova.

He looked as though he'd seen the Devil, and maybe that was explanation enough.

But they weren't rid of the woman, not even when they came out in their black leotards and tights and began to warm up with the other dancers. As Layla and Sean stretched, Margo watched. She was clearly used to being the top dog (*Or top bitch*, Layla thought) in any room. Layla noticed there was a vampire following Margo everywhere she went; he wore a suit and tie, he was heavily muscled, and he looked extremely bored. Margo's bodyguard.

I'm not surprised she needs one, Layla thought. A cold tendril of anger wound through Layla's heart. The more Margo watched Sean, the more the woman discarded the veneer of propriety. Her eyes were greedy, avid, as if Sean was hers for the taking. Layla thought, *She's stalking Sean just like Carver Hutton stalked me. I could kill her for this.*

And the thought of killing Margo didn't seem strange at all.

"Who is she?" she asked Sean, in a voice so low only another vampire could have heard it.

"Margo DeCordova," he said, his face blank.

Layla had an impulse to knock Sean to the floor. "*I know her damn name*," she hissed. "What was your connection to her?"

"We fucked, is that what you want to know?" Sean's unusual outburst made Layla jump. She gave Sean a very flat look.

In a calmer voice, he said, "She is a woman with unusual tastes. I don't want to remember it." He avoided looking in Margo's direction.

Layla saw Sean actually shudder.

*I might not be a great vampire, but I'm not stupid,* Layla thought, *and Margo's trouble.* As the other dancers arrived, their reactions were oddly the same. They gave Margo a startled look, glanced at Sean, and then ignored Margo ostentatiously.

On full alert, Layla listened with close attention to the conversations around her. "...back from Europe," Julie was whispering in Thompson's ear.

The last to arrive, black-haired Abilene, stopped dead when she saw Margo DeCordova. And Abilene's upper lip drew back in a snarl. She spun on her heel and left.

This was a very bad portent, because Abilene cared for nothing and no one besides her partner in their sex performances for Black Moon, which took place in secret little clubs across the city. Her partner's name was Mustafa, and he was very quiet. In fact, Layla had never been sure whether or not Mustafa could speak English.

The room was fairly humming with tension when Margo DeCordova left to take her seat in the auditorium. After she vanished, the fear drained out of the room. Sean sagged against the wall, his eyes closed.

———◆———

SYLVIA DAYTON called, "Everyone crowd around."

Feodor suddenly materialized (had he been avoiding Margo, too?) to give them notes on the previous rehearsal of "Sex, Love, and the Dance." He'd moved Layla and Sean to the last slot, the closing duo.

"Concentrate on each other," Feodor said. "You'll make everyone in the audience think about sex. This is good for Valentine's Day." There was a smattering of laughter.

Layla was glad she had the length of the program to get into her own head, to prepare. While the other dancers went through their own pre-performance routines, she and Sean kept moving and stretching. In the second half of the program, Thompson and Julie's tango was snappy and erotic, and Abilene's technically perfect ballet with Feodor was a real achievement. Abilene's short dark hair and small, slender body contrasted beautifully with Feodor's sleek muscles and fair looks. There wasn't sexual passion in the way the two interacted...but it was picture-book beautiful. Layla gave Abilene a quick kiss on the cheek as she left the stage, and Abilene looked startled, but pleased.

Ten minutes before they were to go on, Sean put his arms around Layla, and he lay his head against hers. It was what they had done every time before they performed this duet. The ritual forced them to put aside all the other stimulations around them. Layla thought about the two of them becoming one: connection, reconnection, the bond of lovers.

Layla's sharpened senses and her awareness of her partner made the ten minutes magical. After days of uncertainty and surprise, she found peace in the knowledge that she was about to do something she did very well. No one could deny that.

"Time," said Sylvia quietly, and Layla was back in her body, her troubles temporarily banished. There was only Sean, and her, and what they would create together. They took their places on stage in the darkness, and the gusty voice of the Andean pipe began, eerie and wailing. The lights slowly came up. And they danced, twining and releasing, sinuous, two halves of one whole.

The applause was almost an anticlimax. Layla bowed, and smiled, and did the expected things, but it was her satisfaction with their work that made her happy. That, and the anger on Margo's face, out in the audience. Surely she would leave Sean alone, now—she'd seen how together Sean and Layla were.

Late that night, within the dark safety of their apartment, Sean made love to her with a special tenderness. "Darling, don't worry, everything will be fine," Sean murmured. "Let's forget our problems for tonight. We're together. That's everything."

Layla thought, *Everything will be all right, after all.* She would find a way to prove herself. Sean would confide in her fully. This temporary rift would be healed.

She snuggled up beside him, feeling blissful at the moment dawn claimed her.

———◆———

LAYLA WOKE as suddenly as she had died. She and Sean always opened their eyes at the same moment. Every night, her first move was to turn to him and smile. As she did tonight. But he was gone.

"Honey?" Layla said, but her voice hit the silence of the apartment with a thud. How could this be? she thought. She thought hard, running various scenarios in her head, trying to come up with one that could explain his absence in a non-alarming way.

Moving as quietly as she could, Layla sat up to look around the bedroom. There was not a whisper of sound aside from her own tiny noises; the slither of one silk pajama leg against another, the slide of her hair against her shoulders. She saw well in the dark, but now she wanted to see perfectly. Silently, she padded over to the doorway to switch on the light.

Sean's pillow was on the floor, and the book he'd been reading, the one he'd placed on the bedside table, had been knocked to the floor.

After a quick glance around, Layla thought the rest of the room seemed the same. Sean's clothes were hung up neatly; he had been a valet in his human life and kept his old habits. His shoes were side by side on the closet floor. She crept into the bathroom. His toothbrush was dry. So was the shower stall.

Still moving silently, Layla entered the living room, veering left to detour to the tiny area that was called a "kitchen." In the small refrigerator, both six-packs of synthetic blood were intact. But turning to face the far wall, Layla noticed that the flat-screen had been knocked off its stand.

Layla felt that cold swell of anger again. She made no attempt to tamp it down, not this time.

She checked the inner door, the first of two between the apartment and daytime intruders. Both doors, which had different keys, were unlocked—not broken. This had been a planned attack. A duplicate set of keys could have been created, or the guards could have been bribed. Either way, this was treachery.

Her first impulse was to go downstairs and kill the doorman. She had no qualms at all, though she didn't know quite how she'd accomplish it. But Layla realized that the day guards—who had to be the ones who'd let this happen—were off duty.

Fine. She would track them down.

Acting on instinct, Layla called Abilene. She was the smartest and the hardest vampire Layla knew.

"Uh-huh?" Abilene asked. She had just woken, too.

"It's Layla," she said. She paused, overwhelmed with her loss and fear. Telling someone made this situation seem more real.

"You called me to tell me your name?"

"Abilene," she said. "Sean is gone."

After a moment of silence, Abilene said, "You mean…he left before you rose?"

"No. I mean someone took him." That was the only possible interpretation of the evidence.

"Someone came into your apartment. In a vampire-owned building. Took Sean, while he slept."

"Yes."

"It would be stupid to ask you if you're sure," Abilene said finally. "But what if he decided to go out to San Francisco to take the job offer?"

*If anything else falls on my shoulders I will collapse.* "Of course," Layla said. "The job offer." Layla's rage grew to encompass Sean, as well as his abductors.

"Maybe you didn't want to relocate? Maybe Sean could have decided it was…time for him to go, to avoid weepy goodbyes?"

"Only if he decided to leave naked," Layla said, proud of how calm her voice sounded. At least she had an answer for that.

"Not Sean," Abilene said. There was a moment of silence. "Okay," she said abruptly. "Call Christoph. He owns your building, right? He's liable for anything that happened to Sean during the day. I'll call some of the others. We'll be there soon."

"Thank you," Layla said, but Abilene had already hung up. Layla started to call down to Rubio, but that would be a waste of time. Instead, she called the owner of the building, a vampire named Christoph Simonson, who was about a hundred and fifty years dead, and a real estate magnate.

He answered on the second ring.

"This is Layla LeMay," she said. "You may not remember, but my husband and I live in your building on Morley."

"Who could forget you?" Christoph said jovially. "You are the fairest of them all. How are you and Sean?"

"Sean was stolen from your building while he slept."

"Impossible! You can't blame me if your man decided to leave you without saying goodbye. Though how any man could walk out on you..."

"I'm going to pretend you didn't say any of that." Layla loosed her rage. "I hope you weren't involved, Christoph."

"Of course not!" Christoph protested, but Layla overrode him. "If you were, I'll tell the sheriff, and he'll descend on you like the wrath of God unless I get to you first. Killing me won't stop the news spreading; I've already shared it."

"Layla, I know the Christoph Enterprises contract guarantees to keep you safe from day entry," Christoph said coldly. "And I intend to honor that contract."

"Great!" she snapped. She paused to gain control of herself. "I expect you to personally interview the people who were supposed to protect us. Someone unlocked the doors to our apartment. You know what that means, Christoph. I want to know who bribed them. I want Sean back. So don't be gentle."

Christoph's voice grew farther away, and Layla recognized that he'd turned from the telephone. She heard him say, "Find the day guards at the Simonson Arms, and bring them to me. And spread some plastic on the floor." Christoph's voice grew louder. "I'll call you after I question them."

"Good," Layla said, and ended the call. At least *that* was in motion.

Although she didn't want to do anything but pace back and forth, Layla ran into the bedroom to pull on her clothes and wash her face. In less than ten minutes she was ready for action, her hair braided to stay out of her way.

By the time Abilene knocked, Layla's hands were shaking with anxiety.

Abilene had brought Mustafa, her partner on stage and also in real life. Abileene called him "Moose," because he was a huge and muscular man.

To Layla's astonishment, Thompson came in on their heels, followed by Feodor. Layla was glad to see both of them, but was also surprised that they'd cared enough to come. And she was even more surprised when Rick and Phil followed. Rick was Phil's keeper, lover, and protector. Phil was divinely beautiful, perhaps fifteen in appearance, and he'd always been fond of Layla. Phil was physically as strong as any vampire, but he was very fragile mentally. His life had been hard, and even his death hadn't freed him from an episode of abuse.

Layla felt a flare of hope. Moose was a human, but he was incredibly strong for a non-vampire, and he would do anything Abilene told him to do; and Abilene herself was a stone killer. Thompson was an asshole, but he was never afraid. Though Layla didn't know Feodor well, he'd impressed her as an old-school vampire; he wouldn't hesitate to kill and dispose of a human if it suited his purpose. And she was touched that Rick and Phil had shown up. Rick never let Phil out alone; Phil had no limits when he was angry.

"Thanks for coming so quickly," Layla said. "If you need blood, there's synthetic in the refrigerator. Here's the situation: when I woke up today, Sean was gone. All his clothes are here. His shoes are here. There's no note." She took a deep breath, which she didn't need. "But our doors were unlocked, his pillow was on the floor, a book too, and the television had been knocked over."

"You called Christoph?" Abilene asked.

"Yes. He's going to interrogate the day guards."

"It'll be his ass if something happens to Sean," Abilene said with some satisfaction.

"Yes," said Layla. "It will be."

"Where are Sean's keys? Maybe he walked out in a brand new outfit, and took them with him." Thompson was not sneering, but he wasn't far from it.

Layla went to the bowl on the bookcase by the door. She lifted Sean's keyring and dangled it before them. There was a shamrock charm hanging from ring along with his keys; it had been a gag gift from Julie last Christmas. Layla opened her own small purse, and extricated her own set. She put the two side-by-side on the coffee table.

"So humans came in during the daylight, and they had a copy of your keys," Abilene said.

"Had to have. They took him from our bed, but they left me." Layla was bewildered that only Sean had been snatched.

"I guess you should have been kidnapped, since you're so *pretty?*" Thompson said.

The next thing she knew, Layla was holding him up by his throat.

Vampires weren't often taken by surprise, but all those in Layla's living room were. Even Layla.

No one moved.

Thompson didn't need air, but clearly the pressure of Layla's grip was hurting his neck. He glared at Layla, and his hands began clawing at her arms. But she kept him suspended, and she enjoyed every second of it. He could not make her put him down. After she was sure she'd proved her point, Layla let his feet touch the floor. She expected he would counterattack, and she was ready and eager for it; her fangs ran out. But Thompson only stared at her.

"Thompson, I have to know something. Is this some kind of joke? Maybe you decided to goad me into acting like a 'real' vampire? Tell me now. If you lie, I'll kill you." The rage surged through her, and her head felt like it was whirling.

*I have one thing*, she thought. Sean. *And he's gone. I will do anything to get him back. Anything.*

And she thought, *I'm sure going to have to kill a lot of people.*

Thompson twisted his head from side to side to stretch his neck. He said, "I had nothing to do with whatever's happened to Sean."

Layla believed he was telling the truth. She glanced at Abilene, who nodded. She believed Thompson, too.

The phone rang before she had a chance to calm down. "What?" Layla snarled.

"Christoph here," the vampire said smoothly. "I have tracked the guards on duty yesterday. One of my other humans heard them talking about leaving the country. My man at the airport caught them. After some quick and dirty questioning, they've confessed they were bribed by a woman whose name they cannot say. Literally, they can't say it. They're under some kind of compulsion. Their description of the man who paid them matches Don Brewer, Margo DeCordova's bodyguard, and I remember hearing that Sean was Margo's designated victim the last time she was in Rhodes." A scream rose in the background, but Christoph didn't mention it.

"That *bitch*," Layla whispered.

"Please understand that my involvement is at an end. I have honored our contract. You will have new guards tonight, and a year off your HOA fees."

"All right, Christoph." Layla didn't thank him. He had only done what he ought to do. She didn't know if she'd ever see Sean again, but she was getting a real break on their budget.

She hung up and told the other dancers what the building owner had said, though they'd probably been able to hear it.

"Tell me about Margo," Layla said to Feodor. "Last night I could see that there was some big knowledge about her that you all knew, something that included Sean."

"Margo is a sexual sadist," Feodor said in his precise but accented English. Phil looked directly at Layla, and nodded silently.

Layla sat down abruptly. She'd experienced sexual sadism; and the thought that Sean might be going through the same thing, had probably gone through the same thing on Margo's previous visit, made her sick.

"And Margo's at least three-fourths demon." Abilene was serious. "That gives her the power to control most humans, as well as a few vampires."

Again, Layla realized that she was lagging behind on learning about her new world, the vampire world. There were demons, they had power, and Sean was in the hands of one who liked to hurt people. "He'd been with her before. The way she looked at him, I could tell she wanted him back." She rubbed her face with her hands.

Feodor's face was calm, but his hands were clenching and unclenching. "Many years ago, I was her prey. I can't say it was all bad. At the beginning, I was having a wonderful adventure. Toward the end I didn't amuse her any more, however, and she turned to torture to keep things interesting. For her."

Moose put his huge hand on Feodor's shoulder.

Abilene explained, "Moose had an episode with Margo, too."

"So how old is Margo? That's a lot of sex adventures," Layla said. She didn't feel guilt that her own virtues had led to Margo's interest in Sean. She was not responsible for the woman's evil.

"She ages slower than most humans," Feodor said. "She had me over a hundred years ago. But I still remember it much more clearly than I want to. If I hadn't believed Margo to be in Europe, I wouldn't have answered Sylvia's invitation to come to Rhodes."

"Moose was five years ago." Abilene leaned against her partner, her arm around his waist. "She left for Europe because she had damaged him so badly. He was in the hospital. She was scared of the consequences."

"You didn't strike back?" Layla was incredulous.

"That was before my time," Abilene said. "If we had been together then, I would have killed Margo. I still imagine it when I need to cheer myself up."

"She asked me if she could borrow Phil," Rick said. Rick had his arm around Phil's shoulders. "I told her what would happen if she tried."

"Where does she live?"

"If she's returned to her home, rather than some hotel, she lives on Hartford Avenue," Feodor said. "In a house...well, a mansion."

"Can we do something obvious, like send the police to search her house for Sean?" Layla was grasping at straws.

"Margo can bribe almost anyone," Thompson said. "She married money and she's made money. And since she has so much demon blood, she can compel people to do what she wants them to do. Even some of us. That's why she wasn't arrested for what she did to Moose."

"When I saw her backstage, I could tell that she had acquired more power," Feodor said. "I called a friend of mine in Prague who has connections in demon circles. She told me that Margo had been studying with a renegade witch...and that witch is now shunned by her community."

"I'll go break into her house. And I'll break her fucking neck." Layla paced, unable to stay still.

"You've forgotten something," Thompson said. "You're due on stage tonight. She'll come to you. Margo's sure to be in her seat. She wouldn't miss the first performance. And she wouldn't miss showing her power in front of someone younger and more beautiful." For once, he didn't sound resentful.

"How can I dance without Sean?" Layla was incredulous that anyone could expect this of her.

Abilene put her hand on Layla's arm. "If you aren't there, she'll figure you're too distraught to fight."

"You mean... I have to do this?"

"Yes," Abilene said simply. "Not only will it lull Margo into thinking you're not going to fight for Sean, but you owe Sylvia. We all do. She has organized us, arranged our appearances, and she has set a series of protections in place for us. If she also borrowed money from Margo, well...that's the mistake she made."

"Sean will be shamed if you don't honor your obligation to Sylvia," Thompson said.

Layla looked at each of them in turn. They all nodded, even Moose, even Phil. "Well, if Margo's in the audience, at least she can't be at home torturing Sean. I can't leave him there at her mercy."

"You're going to try to bargain with her?" Thompson asked. The scorn was back on his face.

"I'm going to kill her," Layla said, with bone-deep sincerity.

The room fell silent.

"Well, you've finally bloomed," Thompson said. "Took you long enough."

"If you're not willing to help me, you can leave now."

Rick said, "That's why we're here."

"All of us want to kill her," Abilene told Layla. "We didn't know if you'd reached that point yet. Sean pampered you."

Layla started to dispute this, but realized it was true, and at this point it made no difference. "I need two things. I need a witch, one who's shunning Margo. That shouldn't be too hard to find. And I need a partner for tonight."

Not completely to Layla's surprise, Feodor stepped forward. "I can partner you. I know the routine."

"It's very exacting," Layla said. "The timing has to be perfect, or we'll both look like fools."

"You are telling my grandmother how to suck eggs. I danced with the Bolshoi," Feodor said with dignity.

Layla was unsure how that would qualify him for a sex-drenched modern number, but she could not turn him down. "Great," she said. "We need to practice right now. At the studio." Though it was the last thing she felt like doing, both she and Feodor could be injured if they missed a hold.

"Since you're sure she'll come to lord it over me, we'll have to get her then, though it would be helpful if someone would go to the mansion and make sure she actually drives out tonight. When she comes to the theater…" Layla outlined a sketchy plan.

Abilene said, "I know a witch. I'll call her. And I'll make sure you're armed."

Thompson began calling the other troupe members to tell them what had happened, and what they could expect tonight.

Layla grabbed up everything she would need, and she and Feodor caught a cab to the Blue Moon studio. They had just enough time to get in a rehearsal before the performance.

A CD of the Andean pipe music was there, and Layla, in leggings and a T-shirt, assumed her starting position on the floor. It felt strange and wrong to look up to see Feodor instead of Sean; even more wrong to feel his larger hands on her body in the grips that she'd only practiced with one person. Layla couldn't make a connection with Feodor: she knew that they were going through the motions correctly, but there was no fire. This duet was nothing without passion.

"We have to do better than this," Feodor said, his accent more marked. "You have to feel something for me."

"All right," Layla said. "Hit me. Or kiss me."

Feodor chose the kiss. He was taller than Sean, and smelled different, and held her differently. But Feodor could kiss, and he gave it everything he had.

When they broke apart, Layla could see that Feodor was pleased. "Now we can do this," she said. "Now I feel something."

She felt like she couldn't stand Feodor. But he didn't need to know that. He smiled and gave her a little bow.

Thirty minutes later they were at the auditorium, putting on the plain black stretch outfits for the number. Everyone changed in the same room; there was no modesty among the vampires, and that indifference had come to encompass the human dancers, too. As Layla put on her ballet slippers, she listened to progress reports.

Abilene said, "It was really easy to find a witch who was happy to discover Margo's current location. Clemence is standing by in the dressing room: woman in her fifties, gray hair, purple sweater."

"What does Clemence need to do the job?"

"Proximity. That's what we need, too. We have to lure Margo backstage. I don't think that will be any problem. She'll want to show off. Clemence will counteract any spells Margo attempts."

"In the meantime?" Layla asked.

"Moose went to the DeCordova mansion. He just called. Margo's limo is pulling out. She's definitely coming to the theater."

After a few minutes, the ensemble in the orchestra pit began to play an overture. The dancers huddled together in a cluster, and they all wound their arms together.

"Strength, Layla," whispered Abilene.

The bright music came to a halt. From the stage, Sylvia gave a little speech about the close ties between love, sex, and the art of dancing. She said, "I guarantee if you don't see the connection now, you will when this evening is over." The audience laughed, and settled in to see something unique.

The program began with a waltz. Karl and Megan seemed to float across the stage. Megan, a human, looked beautiful in a full-skirted chiffon gown. Karl, a vampire, was classically handsome in a tux. It was a lovely routine, dreamily romantic. The dancers could practically hear the audience react with a syrupy "Awwww."

The progression from romantic to sexual crept forward, in keeping with the Valentine theme. Team after team performed, some of six dancers, most of two.

After Abilene and Feodor finished their ballet, Abilene took her bow and made a graceful exit into the wings. She dropped the elegance and seized Layla by the shoulder. "Listen," Abilene said. "Don't lose your shit. The bitch brought Sean with her."

Layla felt as if the ceiling had fallen in on her. "How does he look?" she said.

"Frozen," Abilene said. "I can't tell if it's witchcraft, or if she's threatened some terrible reprisal if he…" She paused.

"If he gets up and screams, 'This woman tortured me!'" Thompson said, finishing her thought. "More likely, Margo threatened Layla."

"Let's see how that works for her." Layla hardly recognized her own voice. "She thinks I'm weak. She'll let me get right up to her. She'll want to wave Sean in my face. That's why she brought him."

Feodor at her side, Layla stood like a statue in the wings. Her new partner was intelligent enough not to speak. Layla's thoughts were concentrated on rescuing Sean.

She knew it was time for her to let her new nature go free from all restraint. She was no longer human. She had to act like the vampire she'd become. Layla could control her own future, independent of anyone else. It seemed that she had been able to remain tethered to her former life by the insulation of Sean's care.

Sylvia came to stand beside her. "I heard about Sean." She looked guilty. "I'm sorry."

Layla turned her face to Sylvia. "I'll get him back in time," she said.

"In time?" Sylvia was clearly taken aback; this was not the reaction she'd anticipated from Layla LeMay.

*Yes. In the next thirty minutes.* "I understand he has another job offer?" Layla said conversationally, and Sylvia flinched.

"I didn't realize that you didn't know all about it," she said.

"Sean and I haven't really discussed it." Layla's voice was eerily calm.

"He has a chance to open his own dance school in San Francisco," Sylvia said. "An old friend of mine asked me for a recommendation. And since the, ah, honeymoon year, with you and Sean…was almost over, he was thinking about taking the job as a contingency plan. If you two found you couldn't…"

"Yes." Layla couldn't bear for Sylvia to falter on.

At the moment, the dance was imperative. It would be the first time Sean had seen her from the audience, she realized with a jolt. She glanced in the backstage mirror. She did not look grieved, furious, or in limbo. Her face was under control. She was ready to dance.

Feodor took her hand. "Remember, you can't look out. Do not falter, woman. If you spook Margo, she'll take him away."

"Yes," she said. *Head up, chest out, shoulders square, big smile, pretty hands.*

On the darkened stage, they took their positions.

When the spotlight came on, Layla lay on the floor clinging to Feodor's leg, her back to the audience. Face forward, Feodor was looking down at her with unmistakable possessiveness. For a long moment, the auditorium fell silent, and the piping music started its breathy sound. Then Feodor reached down to pull Layla up and in one smooth movement she was on her feet and turned. Their faces were side by side, the glacially handsome Russian and the beautiful American. The audience gasped audibly.

Layla moved from Feodor's waist to his shoulders and then she was up in the air, Feodor effortlessly lifting her to sail in the air, and all the while she was reminding herself not to look out. She wound around Feodor in the performance of her life. She never took her eyes from him, and his never strayed from her.

The message of the duet was entirely different with Feodor as her partner. Her body said, "I can't let you go, though I want to," rather than "I will never let you go."

When they took their bow, the applause was tumultuous. Under other circumstances, Layla would have felt proud. But as she smiled and acknowledged the audience, she looked at Sean. Seeing him wiped away every emotion other than pain. He was sitting by Margo, dressed in a suit and tie. His face was blank, and his shoulders sagged.

With a supreme effort, Layla kept smiling, and she did not release Feodor's hand. If she had wondered whether she had enough guts to get Sean back, she doubted no longer.

Once she and Feodor were in the wings, she waited at a gap in the curtains to see what Margo would do. "Feel secure enough, bitch?" Layla whispered. "I am such a wimp, I can't hurt you, right? I betrayed Sean tonight. I danced with someone else! You want to bring him back here so you can parade him in front of me. And Feodor."

Layla barely registered meeting Clemence, though she did see that Clemence approached her very slowly and carefully. But Layla could feel the witch's power. "Do anything to her you can," she said.

Clemence nodded calmly. She looked like anyone's grandmother, in a fuzzy home-knit sweater. "I look forward to it," she said. "Her teacher is cursed among us."

"I am going to kill her," Layla said.

Clemence nodded again. Then she melted into the background. *Like magic*, Layla thought, feeling a smile pull her lips up.

"Abilene," she said, "can you bring me my jacket?"

"Here," Abilene said. She was still wearing her tutu, and she looked fragile and doll-like. She had Layla's jacket, a cheap denim one, over her arm. Layla slid into it carefully. She didn't want to cut herself with the stiletto Abilene had taped inside.

It was lucky she'd been quick, because some of the patrons took advantage of their privileged status to come backstage to congratulate the dancers. Layla, standing side by side with Feodor, gave each one a brilliant smile and said, "Thanks so much!" over and over.

After an interminable wait, Margo de Cordova finally appeared, Sean in tow. Layla felt Sean's presence before she saw him. He looked...stretched tight. When his eyes met hers she read hopelessness. He shook his head in answer to Margo's tug on his arm. He clearly didn't want Margo to approach Layla.

But Layla had been sure she wouldn't need to make a move, and she was right. Margo began making her way inexorably closer, Sean in tow behind her along with the bodyguard—Don Brewer, Christoph had said—who looked bored.

Layla made herself very involved with small talk with Feodor, while the other troupe members began to herd visitors—and the human dancers—back to the dressing rooms. Karl, still in his tux, leered seductively at a middle-aged patron. She looked delighted and willingly followed him back into the wings—out of sight, out of hearing. Well done.

Margo was wearing a small fortune in diamonds and a satisfied look. Don Brewer scanned the area around Layla and Feodor. He didn't seem to be worried about a bunch of dancers, even when Feodor drifted to one side of him, and Thompson to the other.

Abilene was talking animatedly to Moose, who had just walked in with Phil and Rick, other Black Moon employees. Rick held Phil's hand, and Layla could tell that Phil was on edge. His young face had an ancient expression; in his eyes, she could read all the terrible episodes of his life.

"Sean!" Phil said. Layla had seldom heard Phil speak before, and she was surprised at his light voice.

Margo halfway turned, startled but not alarmed, and she did nothing but smile when Phil put his arm around Sean. But when Phil started to lead Sean away, Margo said, "Young man, Sean stays with me tonight."

Everyone was in position. Sylvia was way in the background, and the other patrons were gone.

Layla took a step forward, willing bloody tears to stain her cheeks. "Please let Sean go," she pleaded pathetically, and Margo's face showed both satisfaction and contempt.

"Sean is with me for now," Margo said. "I suppose a new vampire like you is just too insipid for his tastes. Sean, what do you say?" Margo laughed.

Sean tried to speak, but he could not. He looked desperate. That had to be an enchantment, or maybe just Margo's goblin mind-bending. Layla hoped Clemence could counteract it, but at the moment her priority was to move Sean away from his position at Margo's side.

"But I need him," Layla whined, her hands clasped together, and moved closer. Margo didn't seem to fear her at all, and permitted it.

Layla looked over Margo's shoulder at Feodor and Thompson, who were flanking Don Brewer. She nodded almost imperceptibly.

The bodyguard caught the signal and took alarm. Then he glanced from side to side, realizing he was boxed in. It was too late.

Everything happened then: Layla yanked the stiletto from under her jacket, Thompson and Feodor both seized Don's arms, and Phil grabbed Sean and threw him away from the fray, flinging him over to Moose. Margo had time to look livid and to raise her left hand—which gave Layla a perfect target. She slid the stiletto into Margo's heart, her surging strength sliding the blade between Margo's bones as easily as if her flesh had been butter.

Margo looked absolutely astonished in the few seconds before the light went out of her eyes.

Layla smiled.

Before the body could bleed substantially, Layla caught it and held it up, using Margo's evening shawl to absorb the blood. In the next instant, Abilene scooped up Margo's feet. They carried the body over to a dusty width of canvas, part of a long-dismantled set. Within a minute they'd flipped the sides over Margo's body, and Don, seeing his employer was dead, quit struggling. As soon as Feodor and Thompson released him, the bodyguard simply shrugged and walked away.

Feodor and Thompson looked at her questioningly. Should he be released?

Layla wasn't sure if Don had participated in Sean's captivity or not...but he had bribed the men who abducted Sean. In a second she bounded forward, landing high on his back, wrapping his arms to his sides with her strong legs. Layla twisted Don's head until she pulled it off. It wasn't easy as the vampire movies made it seem, and it was quite messy.

But she felt even better after she'd done it, which was strange and interesting.

She tossed the head into the bundle with Margo. It would go to ash soon, anyway.

All this had taken less than three minutes. Sylvia was standing with her mouth open; no sound was emerging.

Layla said, "Sean and I accept the job offer in San Francisco." After a long moment, Sylvia nodded. She leaned against the wall. Her legs were unsteady.

Sean looked almost as rocky. He was standing supported between Phil and Moose.

Layla said, "Phil, I've got him. Thanks so much. You too, Moose." Phil stepped away, a faint smile on his face, and melted into the darkness of backstage with Rick. Abilene leaped onto Moose, who caught her easily. "You are my sweet honey child," she said. He grinned in reply, and carried her back to the dressing room.

Layla gripped Sean's upper arms, to be sure he stayed upright. He sagged against her.

"Can you talk?" she asked.

He shook his head violently.

"Okay, honey. Okay. You'll be all right."

But Sean seemed agitated, and though he didn't push Layla away, he didn't seem as happy, or relieved, as she'd imagined he would.

"He's bespelled," said Clemence. The gray-haired witch seemed quite pleased at the outcome of the evening. "Margo died before she could remove it."

"You think you could have told me that before I killed her?" Layla, still pumped up, had to restrain her impulse to deal out more violence.

"Margo wouldn't have done it," the witch said, shrugging. "But I'll start work. May take me a few tries." She retreated to a quiet corner, and then began to mutter and move her hands around.

Thompson and Feodor carried Margo's wrapped body away from the stage area and down the stairs, directly out the back door to the Blue Moon van. Don the bodyguard had crumbled to ashes. Sylvia, who appeared to be a little steadier, got a dustpan and broom to dispose of him and went in search of a trash can.

Layla didn't care what became of either of the remains. She trusted Thompson and Feodor to dispose of Margo in a safe place.

The building, so full an hour before, had emptied with incredible speed. Through the heavy curtains, Layla could hear the cleaners moving around the auditorium. "Goodbye," Clemence called. "It may take a little time, but he should speak again tonight. If not, take two aspirins and call me...well, in the evening."

Layla was alone with Sean, and he was still propped up against her. She felt she could stand there all night, him leaning on her. She could feel that he was growing stronger.

The moment finally came when Sean was able to step back from her, to look into Layla's eyes.

"While you can't interrupt me," she said, "I'm going to tell you a few new rules."

He raised his eyebrows.

"When you have a job offer, you tell me. When you have a stalker, you tell me. When I need to step up and break someone's bones to establish my strength, *you tell me.*"

Sean nodded emphatically.

"Now," Layla said. "We're going to leave Rhodes, okay? You're going to accept the job offer. And I am going with you. And we will not split up."

When Sean began to cry, she did, too.

Layla had never seen him weep. His short time in Margo's hands must have awakened some terrible memories. But Layla steeled herself and finished what she had to say. "Listen. If you ever, ever disrespect me again, I will take your head off. You know I can do it. Sean, you made me, but I'm not your baby. Don't keep things from me. Don't imagine I can't survive without you. Now, do you understand all that? Because you can go to San Francisco all by yourself if you don't." She felt her ferocity rise again, and the process felt smoother and stronger. Sean could feel it too. He nodded emphatically.

Layla's anger seeped away as she looked into Sean's face. "I'd kill her all over again," she whispered.

Outside the back door, Margo's limousine and driver waited.

Sean glanced at the car, back at Layla, a question in his eyes.

"I'm not telling the driver he doesn't need to wait," Layla said. She shrugged. "Sooner or later, it'll come to him. Wait. Is he the one who drove you over to Margo's? After they took you?"

Sean nodded.

Layla knocked on the chauffeur's window. Startled, he opened the door and said, "Can I help you?"

For the first time, she used her glamor. Looking directly into his eyes, she freed herself to take his will. "You drive back to the nearest police station," she told him. "You're terribly afraid you may have done something awful to Margo after you picked her up from the theater."

The man stared at her, dazed. "I will," he said.

Layla broke eye contact and strode back to the sidewalk where Sean was waiting. She felt strong, she felt capable, she felt like she would never live a passive life again.

"I have a new mantra," she told Sean, as they walked down the cold street.

He pantomimed raising his head, bracing his shoulders, smiling, and holding his hands in graceful curves. Layla laughed.

Sean waited, his eyebrows raised inquiringly.

"Head up, shoulders square, no smile, fangs out," Layla said.

And Sean nodded.